P9-EDU-656

"I have been waiting for this moment."

Edward's voice was as intent as the look in his eyes. "You are warm and full of heart," he continued, "and I am very glad to have you for a friend."

Susanna fought for something special enough to say. "Your friendship is very precious to me. I remember everything we ever said or did together."

"My memories are pleasant, as well," Edward agreed. "But I have a powerful motive for wishing you in the present."

"I am here in the present," she said as calmly as she could.

"Susanna, will you do me the honour?"

"Oh, yes."

"Then allow me to introduce someone to your acquaintance." He gestured widely and smiled at a figure in the doorway. "Susanna, I should like you to meet the young lady I intend to marry...."

LESSONS FOR A LADY

BARBARA NEIL

Harlequin Books

TORONTO • NEW YORK • LONDON
AMSTERDAM • PARIS • SYDNEY • HAMBURG
STOCKHOLM • ATHENS • TOKYO • MILAN

Published March 1990

ISBN 0-373-31121-4

Copyright © 1990 by Barbara Sherrod. All rights reserved.
Philippine copyright 1990. Australian copyright 1990.
Except for use in any review, the reproduction or utilization of
this work in whole or in part in any form by any electronic,
mechanical or other means, now known or hereafter invented,
including xerography, photocopying and recording, or in any
information storage or retrieval system, is forbidden without
the permission of the publisher, Harlequin Enterprises Limited,
225 Duncan Mill Road, Don Mills, Ontario, Canada M3B 3K9.

All the characters in this book have no existence outside the
imagination of the author and have no relation whatsoever to
anyone bearing the same name or names. They are not even
distantly inspired by any individual known or unknown to the
author, and all the incidents are pure invention.

The Harlequin trademarks, consisting of the words
HARLEQUIN REGENCY ROMANCE and the portrayal of a Harlequin,
are trademarks of Harlequin Enterprises Limited; the portrayal of a
Harlequin is registered in the United States Patent and Trademark
Office and in the Canada Trade Marks Office.

Printed in U.S.A.

CHAPTER ONE

DEBUT

SUSANNA MARLOWE stood at the head of the grand staircase, receiving the congratulations of the arriving guests. Nearby, her heavily bejewelled mother endeavoured to smile as she welcomed each lady and gentleman to Edenhurst. Her father compensated for his wife's reticence by giving out with voluble greetings. Inside the ballroom, the sound of lilting violins filled the hall, the table was abundant with flavourful, colourful dishes, and the wine flowed. Whatever could be found in the way of vulgarity and ostentation to celebrate his daughter's birthday, Mr. Marlowe had spared no expense to purchase.

The name of each guest was announced by a footman liveried in scarlet and lace. He stood at a Doric column in the entrance, between the top of the staircase and the ballroom. As he sounded a succession of appellations through his proud nose, Susanna strove to identify the guests who belonged to them. She was too intent on examining the faces of the guests to pay any heed to their stares and smirks.

She knew that her neighbours had come expressly to watch the upstart Marlowes on parade. She knew they wished to see Mrs. Marlowe—the daughter of a miller—squirm in her elevated position. She knew they wished to laugh at Henry Marlowe's love of show. But none of that mattered to her now. What mattered was that she was searching for one face among the guests, a strong, well-formed face, framed with dark hair and rendered expressive by a pair of dark eyes. Whenever another new arrival appeared on the stairs, she felt the start of anticipation, the ardent wish that it would prove to be Edward Farrineau.

After some time spent in this manner, it seemed to Susanna that everybody had arrived. Disappointed at not seeing the only face she wished to see, she moved through the columns at the entrance and stood in a corner of the ballroom. This situation permitted her an advantageous view of the dancers. Perhaps she would discover Edward Farrineau among them. She held to the slender hope that in the crush he had been unable to greet her and had therefore come inside with the intention of paying his compliments later. He was certain to be close by, for she had heard his father say that he meant to put in an appearance at her debut, and that nothing and no one would keep him away.

Not far from the corner stood three young ladies with their backs to Susanna. They were too engrossed in tittering among themselves to admire the dancers on the floor. One of the young women raised a high-pitched laugh. "Oh, the vulgarity of that female!" she cried. "It makes one ashamed of one's own sex."

Susanna recognized the voice of Dora Martin, the daughter of a wealthy landlord.

"If she wore any more gewgaws and trinkets, she would jingle like a cowbell," said another young lady. Her squeal identified her as Mercy Gayle, offspring of a man of property.

Well did Susanna know the laughing Dora and the squealing Mercy. Among the girls in the village of

Cheedham, they had always taken the lead in sneering at her manners and parentage.

"What I wish to know is how it will be possible to keep one's countenance tonight," Dora said.

"It will be difficult, I own," Mercy replied. "One is never easy when laughing at one's hostess behind a fan. Papa says we cannot be blamed for laughing at Mrs. Marlowe, but it does make one feel quite the hypocrite."

Susanna closed her eyes, mortified. She had always acknowledged that her parents lacked polish and were scorned in consequence. Knowing these facts, however, did not make Mercy's words any less painful.

"You are awfully quiet, Lucy," Dora complained. "Have you nothing to say for yourself?"

"I do not laugh at Mrs. Marlowe," answered a soft feminine voice. It came from a young woman named Lucy Bledsoe, with whom Susanna had only the merest acquaintance. "She was most kind once when my brother was ill," Lucy went on to say. "Mrs. Marlowe brought us some apples from Edenhurst and showed me how they might be baked for Laurence in the mildest way."

Dora said querulously, "As you insist on it, Lucy, I shall grant the creature one virtue—that of charity towards the infirm. But if you will defend the mother, you cannot refuse to be appalled at the daughter!"

Susanna's eyes opened wide.

Lucy replied, "I have seen Miss Marlowe in the village once or twice and we were introduced when we were both girls, but as I have lived with my aunt in town these past years, I can scarcely say that I am acquainted with her."

"Oh, but surely you have heard about her," Dora said. "Even though you have been living in London, you cannot have escaped news of her. You must have heard how she tried to kiss a young gentleman."

Nodding, Lucy said, "I had heard that on-dit, but I don't believe it."

Susanna felt a welling of gratitude toward the young lady.

Nettled at Lucy's response, Mercy squeaked, "It must be true. Papa said it was true, and he got it from the vicar who got it from his son."

"Yes, but it does not follow that it *is* true."

In a tone of considerable pique, Mercy said, "My papa says this come-out of hers is a hasty, shatterbrained affair. You will have to confess that it must be so, Lucy, for Miss Marlowe has not had the advantage of a truly genteel education."

Lucy responded tightly, "I expect I have now heard every vicious thing you and Dora could possibly have to say on the subject of Miss Marlowe. Without knowing anything further, I am prepared to take her part." On that, the young woman declared that she could not imagine where her father and brother had disappeared to. In another moment, she excused herself to go in search of them.

When she was gone, Dora Martin was overheard to complain, "Lucy Bledsoe may wish to appear above the rest of us by refusing to acknowledge what is vulgar, but even she cannot be blind to the excesses of the Marlowes."

To which Mercy added, "If Susanna Marlowe has improved since being at school, I shall be very much surprised. Papa says that the daughter of a parvenu can never be anything but a parvenu."

Susanna stepped out of her corner, walked to where the two young women stood and cleared her throat. At the sound, they turned to face her. Her appearance stunned them so profoundly that they could do no more than gape.

Favouring them with a menacing look, Susanna said, "I have not improved so much as to pretend I did not overhear your conversation."

Seeing the gleam in Susanna's eyes, Mercy cried, "Lord save me, she is going to attack us!"

"I shall not attack you here, but if you ever say another unkind word about my mother, I shall waylay you on the lane one day and leave your bloody corpse to be picked clean by insects, birds and rats!"

"I am going to faint," Dora rasped, fanning her neck.

"You will not faint," Susanna commanded. "It will cause a stir. If I wished to mortify my mother and father by causing a stir, I should box your ears. However—" and here she produced a great yawn, "—nothing is so tiresome as a stir. No, you must mind your manners and think what may be done to improve them. You have my leave to go now and pay your compliments to my mother."

The two young women would have hurried away, but Susanna stayed them another moment with a final caution. "You will behave very prettily to my mother. I shall be watching you."

Nodding and shuddering at the same time, Dora and Mercy turned and fled. As Susanna followed them with her eyes, she wished she could feel even the smallest satisfaction in having terrorized them as much as they deserved. Instead, tears of vexation blurred her eyes.

A familiar hand took Susanna's at that moment and pressed it to a pair of lips. Looking up, she saw Edward Farrineau smile at her. After a brief pause, he said, "You are weeping."

Too full in her heart to lie, she said only, "I am glad you are here."

"I should like to think that anticipating our meeting tonight has moved you to this adorable shower of tears, but

I am afraid some cavalier has broken your heart. Tell me who the fellow is, Susanna, and I shall give him my very best set-down."

She could not resist a smile. "I am told you have been in Switzerland all this time," she said.

"I was sent there to study the physical sciences and do what I could toward the enhancement of my character and judgement by living with a family who spoke only German. No doubt you can tell that I am much improved as a result." With that, he clicked his heels and performed a smart bow.

Not only did he appear to Susanna much improved, both in looks and manner, but she was amazed to observe that, since their last meeting, he had become a man. She wasn't precisely sure what she had expected him to become, and, after all, he could hardly be expected to remain a youth forever. But it jarred her to see his dark hair neatly brushed instead of tangled. His bearing was manly, and his long arms and fine large hands suddenly seemed proportional to the rest of him. He spoke easily, with an air of amusement, but when he spoke her name, his tone betrayed a depth of feeling.

She had feared that his education on the continent would give him a disgust of those whose position in society was founded solely on wealth. She had feared that he might have forgotten the many childhood hours they had whiled away together. She had feared that he would greet her, if not coldly, then politely, as though she meant no more to him than any other young lady in the room. But the glow in his eyes told her at once that none of these catastrophes had come to pass, and that he was more than pleased to see her.

In his turn, Edward appraised Susanna, who had grown into a young woman since he had last seen her. She wore a white high-waisted frock, cut in a low square across her bosom. Her transparent puff sleeves, like her hem, were delicately embroidered with yellow rosebuds and pearls. The maid had swept up her reddish-blonde hair in a crown and coerced little curls to come forward around her face. She wore no jewellery except a locket her mother had given her before their getting so far up in the world. And the effect was charming. "You are very beautiful," Edward said.

"And you are very beautiful, too."

He laughed and she blushed.

"I ought not to have said that," she confessed. "Now I am out, I must not tell beautiful gentlemen that they are beautiful."

"You can tell *me*, Susanna. I don't object."

"No, no. You will grow conceited and there will be no enduring you."

"You are afraid I shall think that every woman in the room is in love with me."

"Perhaps they *are* in love with you."

He smiled, certain that she meant to quiz him. "I expect your dance card is already filled. I am too late, I daresay, to engage you for a set."

"You will think me a hoyden when I tell you that I have saved the country dances for you."

He laughed with pleasure. "You *are* a hoyden, but the most delightful one I have ever had the good fortune to know." He added in a serious tone, "I knew I could depend on you not to change, Susanna. In my loneliest, most tiresome moments on the continent, I imagined what you would say to me if you were there, and I always knew you would have supplied something lively and surprising to cheer me." He put her gloved hand to his lips again, then went off to mingle with the other guests.

There was no time to treasure Edward's words. Susanna was immediately escorted by her father into the centre of the hall, where Sir Dalton Farrineau, father of Edward, was granted the honour of leading her down to the head of the set.

SIR DALTON FARRINEAU of Langfield traced his line back to the reign of Henry Tudor. His was not only the oldest family in Cheedham; it was also the first in dignity and consequence. First in wealth, however, was Mr. Marlowe, of the East End in London, where he had prospered very suddenly as an importer. He was known in business circles to have some undefined, though important, connections with commodities grown in the isles of the West Indies and consumed in the isle of Britain. Beyond this, little was known about Henry Marlowe, save the fact that he had removed his family to the country as soon as he had found a house grand enough to let.

Each of the families consisted of a father, a mother and a single, much adored offspring. Edward Farrineau, heir to Langfield and its lands, estates and cottages, was the centre of his father's hopes for the family and the nation. Sir Dalton regarded his son as the most perfectly formed, well-featured, athletic and quick-thinking human creature ever to have lisped the word "Papa" a sevenmonth after his birth. Lady Farrineau's sole regret was that Sir Dalton was only a knight and therefore unable to pass a title down to their son.

The Marlowes adored their daughter fully as much as Sir Dalton and Lady Farrineau idolized their son, but Mrs. Marlowe regarded her child without blind partiality. She saw in Susanna a spirited girl who was not likely to be tamed by her sudden elevation to a stratum of society so unlike the one in which she was born. For herself, Mrs.

Marlowe cared little about magnificent houses and fine
equipages and did her best to ignore the murmurings and
sniggerings of her neighbours. If they wished to laugh at
her heaps of jewellery and her want of style, she was good-
natured enough to wish them pleasure in their gossip.
When it came to her daughter, however, she was a mother
bird, guarding her tender chick, ready to dive at any creature that threatened its well-being. Unfortunately, she had
had much cause to peck at her neighbours over the years,
for Susanna had fallen into as much mischief as a mouse
in a box of Stilton cheese. The girl had been accused of
attempting to kiss the vicar's son. Fortunately, that charge
had never been proved, but Mrs. Marlowe did know for a
fact that her daughter, at the age of fifteen, had gone so far
as to dress up like a boy and attend a mill in Tewkesbury.

Only one thing caused Mrs. Marlowe more anguish than
her daughter's scrapes, and that was the knowledge that
she must outgrow them. Once that occurred, Susanna
would look to become as fine as the ladies who now made
her the object of their sneers. The instant that desire took
hold, her daughter would be lost to her.

When the Marlowes had first entered the county, Sir
Dalton had consented to be introduced to Mr. Marlowe's
acquaintance and was heard to say that he was glad someone had at last taken Edenhurst to let. But he did not mean
to know the fellow, who, after all, was a nobody, and a
vulgar one to boot. Mr. Marlowe's excess of heartiness,
undiscriminating laughter and slaps on the back must offend any gentleman of taste. Worse, he let his young
daughter roam the village at will, without proper chap-
eron or governess to guide and protect her.

Two subsequent events soon changed Sir Dalton's mind,
however. The first of these was Mr. Marlowe's renovation
of the handsome, though neglected, Edenhurst estate.

When Sir Dalton paid the call that duty forced him to pay and found the renovation as gaudy as he had feared, all his convictions regarding his own taste and elegance were confirmed, and he discovered that it was singularly convenient to look down upon the neighbour whose riches he could not help but envy.

The second event was Sir Dalton's recent attainment of a knighthood following his service to the King in a matter of delicate negotiation with Mr. Andrews of the United States, Mr. MacHolly of Canada, and Mr. White-Horned Stag of the Mohawk Indian Tribe. As Mr. Farrineau, it had been quite impossible for him to allow anything approaching an acquaintance with the likes of Henry Marlowe, but as Sir Dalton he was obliged to assume a posture of condescension towards those of inferior rank. Knighthood carried with it a responsibility to exert the force of leadership in a neighbourhood, and Sir Dalton, humbled by this new responsibility, resolved to use his influence in the cause of universal harmony.

IT WAS IN THIS SPIRIT of harmony that the knight danced the first dance with Susanna Marlowe at her debut. Whatever he may have heard or thought about her past career appeared to have been forgotten. He spoke on indifferent subjects: the weather, the birthday, the delightfulness of the party. His gallantry moved Susanna as she searched the gentleman's countenance for points of resemblance to his son. Then, afterwards, when Edward approached to claim her for the country dances, Sir Dalton bowed and handed her over with all the geniality of a true English gentleman.

"Your father has been so very kind," she said.

"Since his being knighted, he is always kind," Edward replied.

"Not always. Once I believed he would never forgive me."

"Which of your escapades did you think would make him your enemy?"

"I have never seen anyone as angry as he was when I chased away his partridges."

"If I recall, Susanna, he merely handed you a lecture. I should have done a good deal more than that if you had come upon me just as I was on the point of taking a shot."

"I suppose he meant to bag half a dozen of the poor creatures."

"He did not mind losing a few partridges. What overset him was your leaping so close to the line of fire. That was foolish, and you know it."

"Yes," she said with a mischievous look, "but I did succeed in frightening the partridges away."

He shook his head, smiling. Then, taking her hand, he led her onto the floor, where they joined the set. As he turned her sedately under his arm, he said gravely, "You must allow me to offer my condolences."

Feeling the strength of his hold on her hand and looking into his eyes, she could not imagine why she should merit sympathy now, when she was as happy as it was possible to be. "How can you pity the most fortunate creature in the world?" she inquired.

"Now that you're grown up, you will have to give up defending the partridges. You will have to give up all the happy misadventures."

"Oh, must I give them up? Can't you grant me a small misadventure allowance, just as Papa gives me an allowance of pin money?"

"*I* certainly can, but I fear the world cannot. It wishes you to comport yourself as a lady should. Will you mind very much?"

"I shall do well enough. I have been to school in Worcester, and while I have not imbibed every stricture my teachers strove to teach, I have learned that a young lady doesn't require partridges to amuse herself. She has at her disposal a host of diversions."

"Does she? And what are they?"

"Falling in love, breaking gentlemen's hearts, breaking other young ladies' hearts, breaking her own heart. The variety is endless."

"Whose heart will you break first?"

"My own, of course. There is nothing to compare with a broken heart of one's own. It is a great source of lively occupation and keeps one's thoughts engrossed better than any romance of Fanny Burney's."

He stopped dancing to look at her seriously. "I cannot permit you to break your heart," he said. "I am too fond of you to see you indulge in such a misadventure as that."

Gratified at this warm expression, she could hardly find the breath to go on dancing.

"Come," he said. "I can't hold off a minute longer. Come with me."

So saying, he took her hand firmly and led her to the wide French doors that opened onto the balcony. Unnoticed by the dancers, they slipped outside into the evening air. For a moment they inhaled the fragrance drifting up from the rose garden. Then taking her by the shoulders, Edward turned her to face him.

"Susanna, I have been waiting some time for this moment."

She did not move or speak, waiting for him to go on.

"You'll think I'm a perfect dolt for making such a fuss, but ever since I was sent abroad—ever since we were parted—I've had it in my mind to do this."

It was an effort to swallow. She, too, had thought much and miserably about their separation, and the first wish of her heart had been to see him again.

"Now, at last, I can tell you," he said.

"Oh, Edward, you have forgiven me!"

He regarded her a moment. "Forgiven you for what?"

"For quarrelling with you so abominably. Don't you recall that we had words, dreadful words, and were obliged to part before we could patch it up between us?"

"Did we quarrel? Good heavens. What about?"

"Julius Caesar."

He laughed.

Vexed at his amusement, Susanna said, "Surely you remember I said that he was cold and heartless and I would never want to have him for a friend. That was what set you off."

"Well, I am glad to hear we quarrelled over something important. I should be desolate to think that we parted in anger over nothing." Then his smile faded as he added, "But you are warm and full of heart and I am very glad I have you for a friend."

The heat these words produced in her cheeks caused her to put her hands to her face.

His gaze was intent. "Let us not speak of the past."

"The past is very precious to me. I remember everything you ever said."

"My memories are pleasant as well, but I have a powerful motive just now for wishing you in the present."

Meeting his look, she clung to the strength of his voice. "I am here in the present," she said as calmly as she could.

"Susanna, will you do me the honour?"

"Oh, yes."

"Then allow me to introduce someone to your acquaintance." He gestured widely and smiled at a figure standing in the doorway. "Susanna, I should like you to meet Miss Lucy Bledsoe, the young lady I intend to marry."

CHAPTER TWO

THE SCANDAL

THE YOUNG LADY in the doorway walked forward with her hand outstretched and a warm smile illuminating her lovely face.

Susanna looked into Edward's eyes. She found them regarding the young woman with a glow that sank her utterly.

"It means a great deal to me that the two of you should become friends," Edward told Susanna, "for you are more important to me than any two women in the world."

He stood back, waiting to see them greet each other. Susanna found herself face-to-face with the young woman who had defended her to Dora Martin and Mercy Gayle. Ordinarily, Susanna would have been gratified beyond expression to meet her champion, but having seen the way Edward looked at Miss Bledsoe, there was no one in the room of whom she had a greater desire to think ill. She studied Lucy minutely. To her despair, she could find no fault with her.

Her elegance in every feature was what struck Susanna most forcibly. In her manners, composure, voice, gestures, pale green gown, sedate diamonds, pink skin—in every possible way, in short—Lucy Bledsoe was simply and completely elegant. She smiled at Susanna, asking if she felt quite well, if something had happened perhaps to dis-

tress her, if there was anything she could do to be of assistance. This kindness was offered with an expression of
such gentleness that Susanna felt humbled.

"I shall take my leave now," Edward said, "so that the
two of you may become better acquainted." He backed
towards the doors to the ballroom and pulled them shut
after him.

"This is very kind of Mr. Farrineau," Lucy said, "to
give up his dance with you so that I may have an opportunity of a tête-a-tête."

Susanna could not reply.

"And why shouldn't he be kind?" the elegant Miss
Bledsoe continued, giving Susanna the opportunity to
collect her wits. "From everything I hear, you have been
his most devoted friend."

This was so excessive a compliment that Susanna could
not let it go unanswered. "Nothing of the sort, Miss Bledsoe," she replied. "His association with me has brought
him only gossip and trouble."

"You must call me Lucy."

"Oh."

"I'm only two years your senior, Miss Marlowe. I can't
be as fearsome as all that."

"You aren't fearsome. You're quite splendid. I wish you
weren't so splendid. But if I am to call you Lucy, you must
call me Susanna."

After studying Susanna's pained look, Miss Bledsoe
stepped back a little and smiled sadly. "You don't wish to
know me, I collect. I confess, I'm a little puzzled and a
good deal disappointed. But I won't press you. As my
presence appears to make you uneasy, I shall trouble you
no further."

"Wait!" Susanna cried, grasping the young lady's hand. "I do wish to be your friend, but I don't have any friends, except Edward, of course."

Miss Bledsoe smiled. "I understand perfectly. Well, you now have two friends. I shall make you better acquainted with Laurence, my brother, and then you will have three friends. Soon you will have a crowd of friends."

Susanna was glad that the cover of night hid her red cheeks.

"I am told," Lucy continued, "that you have known Mr. Farrineau very well all these years. I, on the other hand, had no opportunity to further my acquaintance with him until we chanced to meet last year, when we took my brother to Baden-Baden. At that time, Mr. Farrineau spoke much of you. He says you can testify to the fact that he is not a rackety fellow."

Shocked, Susanna said, "He is not the least bit rackety. Wherever did you hear such a vile humgudgeon?"

"Well, there was a story that the two of you went in swimming together. I suppose it is mere idle gossip."

Susanna blanched. For some time she paced, while Lucy regarded her in bafflement. At last, Susanna found the courage to say, "I am afraid that story is true."

"Good heavens! Mr. Farrineau compromised a young girl's reputation, and in such a manner? I can scarcely credit it."

Susanna sighed. "I believe it was I who compromised his reputation," she said, and with that surprising revelation, she proceeded to unfold the story of the infamous swim.

ON THE BANKS of a sweet stream called the Dance, stood a line of willows with branches leaning so low that they seemed to want to tumble into the gentle water. These willows formed the favourite youthful haunt of Susanna and

Edward, and on that hot afternoon, he reclined against a willow with his head pillowed on his coat and a Latin book open on his chest, while she lay stretched out on a branch, peering down at her reflection in the water and reciting a paragraph from *The Gallic War*.

"Now do you see why I dislike this Julius Caesar of yours?" she asked him. "He is a dreadful man."

"Naturally he strikes you as dreadful. You are thirteen years old and your opinions are founded on ignorance." Four and one-half years older than Susanna, Edward was fully conscious of his superior wisdom. "You aren't going to fall off that branch, are you?" he asked her.

She ignored the last part of this speech. "What has my age to do with anything? You said yourself I was an excellent scholar. The fault is Caesar's, not mine. He says nothing whatever of Diviciacus. Just a few pages before, the poor fellow was his great friend and he could do nothing without him. Now he won't even make mention of his death."

Edward roused himself from his languor. "Caesar keeps strictly to the subject of the war and does not digress upon such matters as who died and when. His brevity and objectivity are two reasons why he stands with the finest writers of the age."

"He is disloyal, that is what he is."

The young man gazed at the sunshine filtering through the leaves. "You never see things as you ought, Susanna. That's what comes of your father's neglecting your education. He ought to hire a governess or send you to school."

"Papa had a governess for me, but she looked down her nose at us and frightened Mama to tears. As to school, he says he made his fortune without it and thinks I have too much spirit to get on with the teachers."

"But something must be done about you."

"Well, you may teach me. That will do for my education."

"I can teach you a bit of Latin, but I can't teach you what young girls ought to know."

"You make it sound such a great secret. I hope it is; I love secrets."

He shook his head. "The truth is, you have no notion of propriety. You do and say whatever comes into your head."

"I know." Here she sighed. "I am very bad. My poor mother despairs of me. She says I will grow up a hoyden. What is a hoyden, Edward?"

"An impudent little girl who cries over dead military heroes instead of attending to her lessons."

"No matter what propriety demands, Edward, if you die, I shall not forget you. I shall always say you were my friend, my best and dearest friend."

Putting his hands behind his head, Edward regarded her with a smile. "Yes, I know you will. And if after I died, someone were to whisper so much as a word against me, I vow you would plant him a facer in my memory."

"That I would. Edward?"

"What now, hoyden?"

"My petticoat is caught on the tree. I can't move."

"I warned you it would be so."

"You were right, but I bear you no ill will for it."

He tossed his book aside, rose from the grass and brushed off his breeches. After estimating the extent of Susanna's predicament, he directed her to inch slowly backwards along the branch. She soon became so firmly caught that she could not move at all. While Edward worked to untangle her skirts on one side, she lost her balance on the other.

Edward grasped her hand. "Hold on."

He might have rescued her had Susanna not suddenly plunged headlong into the water. Because she had obeyed to the letter his command to hold on, she pulled Edward in after her.

The instant he surfaced, he swam to Susanna, who floated facedown with alarming stillness.

"Susanna!" he called, reaching for her.

"Yes?" she answered, lifting her head with a laugh, jumping up and down and splashing him.

"You did it on purpose!" Abruptly, he let her go.

"On my honour, I didn't! But I was thinking that if we could have a swim it would be the loveliest thing in the world."

Wading to the bank, Edward grasped a willow branch and pulled himself up to dry land. "Fortunately, my book is safe," he said, picking up the volume where he had set it on the grass. When he stood up again, he was amazed to look into the thin, scowling face of Mr. Sharpe, the vicar.

"Edward, come back!" Susanna called. "I only meant to give you a share in my swim. You must not go off and leave me alone. This is horribly disloyal. You are as heartless as Mr. Caesar."

Mr. Sharpe moved to the bank and peered over his spectacles into the water, where Susanna disported herself merrily. "Miss Marlowe!" he said, startling her. "Come out at once!"

Instantly, she swam to the edge and was handed out. Her wet skirts clung to her legs; she shivered as a cloud shaded the sun.

Noting that she was chilled, Edward picked up the coat he had lately used as a head cushion and put it around her.

"Mr. Farrineau. Where is your tutor?" Mr. Sharpe demanded.

"Gone to Worcester for the day, sir."

"Then you ought to be at your studies in preparation for the next day's lessons. You will not succeed at Oxford without application. You will not succeed at anything if you fritter away your time with improper associates." Here he fixed a stern eye on Susanna. "You young people will follow me!" No sooner had Mr. Sharpe made this pronouncement than he turned on his heel and stalked up the slope to the path.

"It was all my fault," Susanna assured him as she hurried along in his wake.

"I've no doubt it was."

"No, it was my fault," Edward said. "I was helping her read Julius Caesar when she accidently fell in the Dance."

The vicar froze and turned slowly to face him. "You have presumed to teach this young chit Latin?"

The offensive tone of the question caused Edward to bridle. "She is a fine scholar, sir, and she has had no encouragement to pursue any serious endeavour beyond the barest housewifery."

Summoning all his patience, the vicar answered, "In her station, that is exactly what she ought to learn, and no more. She may attend the parish school if she wishes to learn spelling and sums. But what have young ladies to do with wars and great deeds and such? No wonder she thinks nothing of taking a swim in her clothes. You have filled her head full of Caesar, and the loftiness of the prose has congealed her reason."

Before Edward could protest, Susanna laid a restraining hand on his arm. "Thank you, Mr. Sharpe," she said. "I shall be happy to renounce Caesar. He gives himself airs, and forgets his officers as soon as they inconvenience him by dying."

The vicar could hardly contain his rage. "You dare to impugn the character of Julius Caesar?" he cried. "You, an upstart girl of barely thirteen years, with a nobody for a father and a miller's daughter for a mother, you have the temerity to disparage the manners of the noblest general who ever lived?"

"Oh, no, sir. I say nothing against his manners. I am sure he was everything a Roman tyrant ought to be. I only speak of his morals—of which, you will agree, he had precious few."

Raising his eyes to heaven, the vicar collected his emotions. Then, with his teeth grinding audibly, he herded the young people along the path to Langfield.

Some hours later, wearing dry clothing and looking ashamed, the swimmers stood before their fathers in Sir Dalton's study.

Sir Dalton could not refrain from saying to Mr. Marlowe, "I hope you appreciate the gravity of your daughter's situation. It is your neglect of her that has led to this wickedness."

"Wickedness, is it?" Mr. Marlowe laughed good-naturedly. "Why, sir, the entire affair was perfectly innocent."

The man's insouciance shocked Sir Dalton. "I advise you," he said angrily, "not to pass this incident off too lightly. I can assure you that the world will not pass it off; nor will it overlook the plain fact that your daughter and my son were found swimming alone together. You may say that they are merely children, but the world will say that they are old enough to produce children of their own!"

Susanna gazed at Edward and he at her. Both felt strangely conscious. She was astonished to learn that Sir Dalton regarded her as a young woman, not a child. She wondered if Edward, too, had ever seen her in that light.

Of late, she had become aware of certain changes of a physical nature that had suddenly rendered her life far less convenient that it had previously been, but she had put these changes out of her mind. Now, however, she began to wonder if she would ever be allowed to forget them.

Mr. Marlowe shrugged. "Susanna is a good lass, has a good heart and if she wants proper behaviour, why, sir, she is only thirteen and has my leave to enjoy herself a little, for she will find herself grown up soon enough. And as to your son there, I'm much obliged to him for teaching my girl Latin because I've got all I can do to know my own lingo. You're a good lad, Mr. Edward Farrineau, and I trust Susanna knows what sort of friend she has in you, but as your father don't like it, I advise you not to do any more swimming with her."

Edward's heart went out to Susanna for endeavouring to shoulder the blame. He also felt aggrieved for his father, who had never found cause before to be ashamed of his son's behaviour. His common sense told him that despite the impropriety of the man's expression, Mr. Marlowe had aptly characterized the episode as innocent. He searched for a means to alleviate the general discomfort and, to that end, asked Mr. Marlowe to put off further discussion of the matter until another time when they should all be in better command of themselves.

As her father led her away, Susanna looked over her shoulder. With her lips, she framed the word *valere* to Edward, and prayed that by her mental declension of the Latin verb meaning "to be strong," he would be infused with all the fortitude necessary to endure a private interview with his sire.

The mishap immediately became known throughout the county, and as Sir Dalton had prophesied, it was viewed throughout Cheedham in the most scandalous light. Mr.

Martin gave it as his opinion that the youngsters ought to be whipped as an example to the other children in the neighbourhood. Mr. Gayle sent his daughter Mercy on an extended visit to her grandmother in Sidmouth so as to ward off any possible contagion from the swimmers. Edward was sent to Oxford a term earlier than originally planned, and thus rescued from the noxious influence of a tradesman's daughter, he was safely ensconced among undergraduates who immediately introduced him to a life of carousal in London's seediest gambling hells. Susanna was enrolled in Miss Wortle's School in Cheedham, where her instructress taught her spelling and drawing but failed to inculcate a single precept regarding the conduct proper in a young lady due to inherit forty thousand pounds.

WHEN SUSANNA CONCLUDED the tale, she waited to see what Lucy Bledsoe would say. She was not above wishing that the elegant young lady's sensibilities would have sustained so severe a shock that she would be forced to decamp on the spot. But Lucy clapped her hands together and said, laughing, "I am sure it must be the most interesting event ever to have taken place in Cheedham. How grateful the villagers must be to you for providing so much lively entertainment."

Susanna sighed. It appeared that Lucy Bledsoe was as liberal-minded as she was kind, beautiful and elegant. Susanna saw that she would have no choice but to admire Miss Lucy Bledsoe and wondered how she could possibly endure it. Happily, she was not called upon to endure it for long, for just then a noise went up in the ballroom and the music ceased playing. The two young ladies looked at each other in alarm, and Edward appeared at the door wearing a grave expression.

"Something has happened," Miss Bledsoe said. "I hope no one is ill."

Susanna, whose first thought was for her mother, threw open the doors and dashed inside. There she saw the crowd of guests murmuring. Her father stood by a painted pillar, expostulating with a white-faced fellow who did not look to be quite a gentleman and who waved his arms and spoke rapidly. Next to her father stood Mrs. Marlowe, Sir Dalton and Mr. Cox, the lawyer.

She felt Edward press her hand. "Do you wish me to come with you?" he asked.

"No." Straightening her shoulders, carrying her chin high, Susanna swept across the floor to stand by her father's side.

"Permit me to take you away," Sir Dalton said.

"I shall stay," Susanna insisted. She listened as her father's interlocutor choked on the word *fraud*.

"I shall set sail for the West Indies at once," said Mr. Marlowe.

"That would be ill-advised," the lawyer argued. "Your leaving England now will be tantamount to an admission of guilt."

"Moreover, there are those who will wish to investigate this matter," Sir Dalton interjected. "They will require your testimony in sorting out the business."

Mr. Marlowe looked from one gentleman to the other. His smile was apologetic, but his jaw was firmly set. Turning to his daughter, he said, "Susanna, puss, you will look after your mother. You will be very poor, I'm afraid, but I shall make it up to you as soon as I may. There's a good girl."

Before the others could prevent him, he strode from the hall with his associate running after him.

Sir Dalton, wearing an expression of the blackest gloom, begged Mrs. Marlowe to do something. "My dear lady, your husband's reputation is sinking every minute. He will be called speculator, fraud, villain and every conceivable epithet. If he should leave England now, his good name will be beyond saving."

"My husband does not ask my advice," Mrs. Marlowe answered. "Nor does he accept it."

"I only ask that you do your best to prevent any harm to your daughter."

The mother regarded Susanna with brimming eyes.

"She is so very much improved," Sir Dalton said. "Her air, her manners, her good nature have begun to be brought out to the greatest advantage. One day, she may take her place in society alongside the most respectable young ladies. If you love her, you will not let her lose her position and respectability. You will speak to your husband and persuade him to remain in England."

Mrs. Marlowe wished to think rationally but a confusion of emotions filled her head. The single idea that remained clear to her was that in this sudden ignominious fall lay the salvation of her motherhood. Scandal relieved her of the duty to promote Susanna's aggrandizement. It meant the girl would not be accepted in society and would not be required to turn her back on an unworthy mother. Surely it was more important for a young girl to have her mother than a position in society. Surely it could not be wrong to keep her daughter by her side instead of tossing her out among the vultures of the world. She loved the girl; the others sneered at her. They would hurt her; she would keep her safe.

Susanna stepped forward to say to Sir Dalton, "If my father believes it is best to go to the West Indies to see to his affairs, my mother and I will not engage to interfere.

We thank you, however, for your kind concern and believe you will ascribe it to the right cause if we must now ask you to excuse us.''

With that, she led her mother from the ballroom, while Sir Dalton, not accustomed to having his advice spurned, predicted that Susanna Marlowe was now ruined forever. The assemblage might have taken pleasure in the prophecy, as well as in the fact that their high hopes for being entertained that evening at the expense of the Marlowes had been answered beyond their wildest expectations. But any such gratification was short-lived, for all thoughts dwelt on the West Indian business that had unaccountably gone awry. There was scarcely a gentleman in the hall who had not in some manner invested in the scheme, and, thanks to Henry Marlowe, every one of them now stood to lose a prodigious amount of money.

CHAPTER THREE

IN DISGRACE WITH FORTUNE

AT THE AGE OF TWENTY-ONE, Edward Farrineau had come into a small but tidy inheritance from his godfather, consisting of a thousand pounds a year, a well-tended farm and an empty house at the edge of Cheedham called Larkwhistle Cottage. It was Edward's intention to place this cottage at the disposal of Mrs. Marlowe. Although he was free to do what he liked with the place, he felt it behooved him to talk with his father about it, not so much because he was inexperienced in deciding matters of property, but because he felt it would please Sir Dalton to be consulted.

Sir Dalton *was* pleased to be consulted, but he was not pleased to learn that instead of renting the cottage to the mother and daughter, Edward meant to give it to them outright. He tried to persuade his son to abandon the idea, saying, "They will never like such a tiny house, not after Edenhurst."

"Mrs. Marlowe is happy to accept the offer of the cottage, Father. She has looked it over and says it will do nicely."

Sir Dalton sighed. "And where does she propose to get the money to live, I ask you?"

"On my last visit to London, I sold some jewels and trinkets for them. Unfortunately, nearly everything else was seized for debt, but the little money I was able to get will allow them to buy a few sticks of furniture and to live without starving.''

Carefully, the knight now broached the subject that troubled him most. ''I'm afraid, Edward, that the world will misconstrue your generosity. A gentleman cannot place a young woman such as Miss Marlowe under that sort of obligation without incurring a great deal of suspicion as to his motives.''

''But Susanna isn't a young woman. She's a girl, my old friend, nearly my sister. If the world wishes to see something sinister in my motives, I can't help it. But I won't abandon her on that account.''

''My boy, what do you suppose Miss Bledsoe will think of your plan? I've known for some time that you harbour hopes in that quarter. You will dash them if you take it into your head to be foolish. When Miss Bledsoe learns of your foolishness, what do you think she will say?''

''I think she will say 'Well done!' because as soon as I told her my idea, she encouraged me to speak to Susanna and her mother straightaway.''

Sir Dalton pondered this news, shocked that such a plan had met with the approval of Miss Lucy Bledsoe, who was as upright in her morals as she was elegant in her dress. But if Miss Bledsoe approved this notion of his son's, it must have some merit, even if Sir Dalton failed to see a particle of it. Reluctantly, therefore, he shrugged and sanctioned Edward's plan for Larkwhistle Cottage, which was just as well, because Edward had already set it in motion.

Susanna was enchanted with the cottage. For one thing, she was charmed by the name, repeating it to her mother and saying with a laugh that the squalling crows on the roof and the squawking cocks they had chased from the sitting room must have frightened off any poor little larks centuries ago.

Mrs. Marlowe, with her daughter's assistance, managed to make the cottage clean and cosy, so that it was not only habitable but also hospitable enough to welcome visitors. Both ladies were perfectly content with it, until Susanna discovered that the cottage was too handy by far to the High Street. Unlike its neighbours, it was afforded no shelter from prying eyes by pretty gardens and vine-covered gates. When the curtains were pulled back to let in the light, every passerby, every inquisitive female, every prying male, every schoolchild, every ostler, hawker and beggar stopped and stared inside the house.

Susanna first noticed she was being stared at one summer afternoon when she sat at her writing table, her chin in her hand and her eyes fixed dreamily on the misty day. Soon she became aware of an array of heads outside her window. Each head bore a pair of saucer eyes that stared at her as though she were a Punch and Judy show or a clown treading the high wire.

"Mama!" she called. "Do you know we are being stared at?"

Mrs. Marlowe did not take her eyes from her mending. "It is better not to notice, dear," she said.

Susanna looked at the crowd again and saw Wilfred Sharpe, the vicar's son, approach the window and poke his nose through the opening.

"How can I help but notice it?" Susanna cried.

"You might close the curtains," Mrs. Marlowe suggested.

"And suffocate? Why should I punish myself and my poor mother simply because my neighbours choose to ogle me in the rudest possible way?"

"I don't know what we can do about it, dear."

Susanna stood up, pushing back her chair. Then, leaning toward the window, she waved Wilfred Sharpe away.

The young wag laughed and waved back. The rest of the crowd followed his lead.

At this impertinence, Susanna shouted, "Go away!"

Wilfred hooted, mimicking her cry of "Go away," and the others followed suit.

"Wilfred Sharpe," she said menacingly, "if you do not go away this minute, I shall have my father bring his army of men from the West Indies and slit your throat."

"I should like it better," Wilfred said so that all could hear him swagger, "if you did the business yourself. I am sure Susanna Marlowe is as likely to slit a man's throat as any savage. However, I should much prefer to have a kiss."

The others applauded his sally, causing Susanna to seize a flowerpot containing a lily in full blossom. After considering her tormentor's grin for a moment, she heaved the pot at him with full force.

The sight of Wilfred's face blackened with soil and his fair hair adorned by a white lily inspired the onlookers to laugh until the tears streamed down their cheeks.

Red-faced with humiliation, he turned an ugly look on Susanna and said in a voice loud enough to be heard over the noisy derision, "I shall not forget who it was that made Wilfred Sharpe a laughingstock." Having levelled this threat, he attempted to stalk through the tittering crowd with dignity, but unable to withstand the jeers, he was at last compelled to quit the scene at a run.

Within the hour, the story of Susanna's encounter with Wilfred was bruited throughout the county. The adventure did little to harm Susanna, for she had long enjoyed a reputation as a hoyden. Wilfred, however, soon found himself greeted on the streets of Cheedham with barely suppressed giggles, and within the space of a day he had become known throughout Worcestershire as "Lily-livered Willy."

"SUSANNA," Edward said during his next visit, "it is said that you rail like a fishwife out your window and threaten to have your neighbours murdered."

"We know, of course, that it's a lie," Lucy added quickly.

"I'm afraid we know nothing of the kind, Miss Bledsoe," Edward gently contradicted. "If you knew Susanna as well as I do, you would inquire carefully before drawing any such conclusion."

"Very well, Mr. Farrineau," Lucy said, "but I can't believe it. I should like to hear what Miss Marlowe has to say."

"I'm afraid it's all true," Susanna said.

"Oh, dear," Lucy murmured.

"Tell us what happened," Edward invited. He had been standing by the cracked plaster mantel and now moved to sit, foreseeing that he was about to hear an interesting story.

"The passersby began to stare at us through the window. Wilfred Sharpe was the rudest of all, for he actually put his face through the opening. Naturally, I told him my father would have his throat slit if he didn't go away."

"Naturally," said Edward.

Having recovered from her initial shock, Lucy smiled a little. "Did you really say that? I should have been too shamefaced to speak. How very brave you are!"

With a good deal less admiration, Edward said, "Susanna, don't you realise that throwing flowerpots at such fellows as Wilfred Sharpe will only win you enemies? He will bear you a grudge for life, I assure you. What is more, you have given your neighbours exactly the satisfaction they sought. You let them egg you on. You let them push you into behaving abominably, and I hope you are sorry for it."

"I'm sorry I threw only a flowerpot at Wilfred."

Edward laughed helplessly. "Miss Bledsoe," he cried, "what are we to do with her? I ask you—look at her." He rose from his chair and walked to where Susanna sat. Then, handing her up, he led her before Lucy, who watched the two of them with the greatest attention. "She is very pretty, is she not? Many red-haired young women are afflicted with difficult complexions, but Susanna's always looks like silk." Here he gestured with his hand so that his fingers almost brushed her fair cheek. "She is neither too tall nor too short, and her figure is extremely tolerable, don't you agree?" Here he held his arm out so that Susanna was able to twirl around under it. "It appears to me that she has the makings of a perfectly delightful female, but when I hear how she behaves, I despair of it."

"You are so very fond of her, Mr. Farrineau," said Lucy, "that I am sure she will listen to whatever you advise in the way of reformation."

"That is the worst of it, Miss Bledsoe. I can't advise her or help her because I delight in her escapades. They make me laugh, which only encourages her wickedness, you know."

Susanna rewarded him with a curtsey and they sat down again.

For some time, Miss Bledsoe remained silent, looking at Edward thoughtfully, and then studying Susanna with equal concentration. At last she spoke, saying slowly, "It seems that Mr. Farrineau wishes to deprive himself of his prime source of entertainment by reforming your manners, Miss Marlowe, and while I think it a pity that he should seek dullness instead of delight, still I must allow that he is right. It won't do, my pretty friend, for you to make yourself ridiculous for the amusement of your neighbours."

Susanna blushed at this characterization of her behaviour. "What do you think I ought to have done?" she asked.

"Nothing," said Miss Bledsoe.

"Nothing? But I've told you how rude they were."

"That is why you ought to have done nothing. Their low manners must not make you rude. In fact, your manners must be of such quality that you disdain to notice another's lack of refinement. You are above it. It cannot touch you."

Susanna looked at Lucy with awe. "Oh, that is excellent! I wish I had done just as you said—looked down my nose and never seen Wilfred at all. Why, he would have felt like the merest fly speck to see me so grand and ladylike."

"Exactly," Lucy said with a smile. "Your politeness would have withered and shrivelled him utterly."

The two young women shared a malicious giggle, while Edward shook his head and then joined them. "It may sound amusing, Susanna," he said, "but it's worth remembering, and not just to make your enemies miserable—though that is a powerful inducement, I own—but to learn to behave like a lady."

"Why should I learn to behave like a lady? I am never to *be* a lady. I am poor, ridiculous and scorned. Such a position boasts few privileges. It boasts only one, in fact—that of behaving badly."

Lucy got up from her chair to sit close to Susanna and take her hands in hers. "No one who knows you, really knows you, believes you behave badly. You have a kind and generous heart and could never do anything truly wrong."

Susanna could not accept this flattering portrayal of herself. "Well, you and Edward don't think I could do anything wrong because you are both excessively good-natured and a trifle blind to people's faults, for which I thank you. But everyone else believes I behave badly."

"Laurence doesn't," said Lucy.

"Your brother?"

"Yes. He has admired you greatly ever since he learned of your swimming adventure."

Susanna glanced at Edward and coloured. "I think he must be funning," she said.

"He has always wished to have a swim in the Dance, but his health does not permit him to. He says you showed remarkable spirit by doing it, instead of just wishing."

"Does he? Well, no one else seems to put such a pleasant face on the matter. I expect your brother is a very agreeable young man. He may visit me, if he likes."

Lucy laughed. "I believe he will like it very much."

LAURENCE WOULD HAVE BEEN enchanted to pay a visit to the spirited Miss Marlowe, but his father would not hear of it. It was one thing for his daughter to have her little charities and to pay visits to the poor. After all, the mother had been most attentive to their family when Laurence was gravely ill, and therefore, it was seemly that Lucy should call on the woman, who was said to be ailing. But it was quite another matter for his son, the heir to an estate of four thousand and the income accruing from lands in Ireland, to call on a young woman of no means, no connections, no prospects and no reputation. She was the daughter of the man who had seduced him into a profitless investment. Furthermore, she was a very model of impropriety, flinging lily pots at the vicar's only son, swimming in her clothes, learning Latin! Mr. Bledsoe did not know when he would recover from the idea of so much impudence gathered together in the person of one young girl.

And so, month after month passed without a visit. The omission was hardly noticed, however, for Mrs. Marlowe's health declined, and at the year's end, she took very ill. After a long winter, when it appeared that the tender care of her daughter, the ministrations of Lucy Bledsoe, and the steady attentions of Edward Farrineau would end by restoring her to health, she died on a rainy day, with her head in Susanna's lap.

AS THE GENTLEMAN of first consequence in Cheedham, as one who had in the past been forced to take a hand in deciding Susanna's fate, and, finally, as a knight of the realm, it fell to Sir Dalton to dispose of Susanna in an appropriate manner. She could not continue at the cottage by herself. The little money she and her mother had lived on would not see her beyond the fall. And Miss Wortle, who acknowledged that Susanna was more qualified than anyone she knew to teach Latin to the children, refused to sully the reputation of her school by employing a young woman of no family or character.

Sir Dalton's duty regarding Susanna was made inordinately difficult by the fact that his son objected to every alternative he suggested. Edward did not wish to see her sent away to become a governess; nor could he permit her to stay in the county and live in the workhouse. But there was little else that could be done with a young woman of nearly nineteen years of age with no husband or father to support her and nowhere to go. Sir Dalton was very much afraid that Edward would take it upon himself to support her, and he believed that would be the ruination of his son's reputation and marital hopes. Therefore, he sent Edward to London on business.

Ordinarily, Edward would not have left Langfield at such a time, but the young man was eager to visit the chambers of a solicitor who might be able to claim certain of Mr. Marlowe's funds for Susanna. If such funds could be obtained, Susanna would have an income of her own and need not be dependent on anyone.

As soon as Edward was gone, Sir Dalton sat down in his chair by the fire to consider what to do about the girl. Although he wanted to be fair and just, he could not help recalling the numerous instances when Susanna had been a trouble to him. He feared she would be trouble to his son and Miss Bledsoe as well. Moreover, he told himself, Edward's unaccountable loyalty would only end by doing the girl harm. What she needed was less coddling and more instruction in morals and manners. What she needed was not to have her own way in everything but to learn how to submit to the better judgement of others. Sir Dalton asked himself how best to accomplish these lofty ends, and he concluded after painstaking reflection that she could not do better than to become Mr. Sharpe's housemaid, a suggestion the vicar had made purely out of charity, despite the spiteful treatment his son had received at the hands of the girl.

"THERE YOU ARE!" said Wilfred Sharpe with an angelic smile. "I thought you would still be dusting in the library. It always takes you a long time to dust in the library because you read more than you dust." Here he laughed, delighted at his own wit.

"You'd better stand away, sir, or you will get wet." Susanna swished the mop so that the water sprayed everywhere.

Wilfred hesitated. He was wearing new breeches and did not wish to get them stained, and he knew Susanna well enough to know that she would like nothing better than to stain them. Hence, he essayed a more conciliatory approach. "Miss Marlowe," he said carefully, "may I be permitted to ask you a question?"

"I am powerless to prevent you."

Grinning, he continued, "Why must we always be at loggerheads? Could we not be friendly?"

Susanna looked up from her task to eye him sceptically. "Was it friendly of you to ogle my mother through the window and to induce our neighbours to do likewise?"

"It was an innocent joke. You cannot think I ever meant any harm. I have always held you in the highest esteem."

Resting her chin on the mop handle, Susanna said, "I do not know whether I ought to believe you."

"But you must know I am your devoted friend. Why, I have even prayed for you!"

She smiled mischievously. "I can say truthfully that you have figured in my prayers as well."

"Have I?" he said with satisfaction.

Susanna went back to her mopping. "Stand away, sir. You will get wet, I promise you."

At this, Wilfred lost patience with friendliness and strode towards her. He grasped the mop handle so that Susanna was unable to continue her work. Looking into his face, she wondered what Lucy Bledsoe would do at such a moment. Would Lucy ignore him? Would she gaze loftily away? Would she reduce him to less than nothing by her dignified scorn?

Susanna decided that this was an auspicious moment to try out ladylike behavior. Accordingly, she sniffed the air, frowned as though it contained a hint of rotting fish, lifted the pail and mop and glided across the room to an unwashed corner.

Wilfred followed her, saying, "You owe me a kiss, Miss Marlowe. You once threw a lily pot at me and gave me a name I abhor to mention. Now you must make it up to me."

Susanna could not understand what she had done wrong. Surely if she had applied Lucy's method correctly, Wilfred would have taken himself off by now. But here he still was, plaguing her as he had done before.

Her only recourse was to try again. This time, she assumed an air of aloofness, as though she were lost in a trance. Turning a curt shoulder on him, she mopped in the most haughty fashion she could contrive.

He came close to her. "You mean to tease me, I see. Very well, Miss Flirt, but I shall have my kiss."

With her outstretched hand, she stopped him. "You will have no such thing. What is the matter with you, Mr. Wilfred Sharpe? Are you blind, deaf and insensible? Don't you see that I am ignoring you in a ladylike manner?"

Pausing, he allowed that, yes, he had seen it.

"Well, do you not know that when you see such politeness, it is incumbent upon you to go away?"

He laughed, a wicked laugh that belied his angelic face. Sliding his hand around her waist, he pulled her to him, murmuring, "I burn to have what is owed to me."

Out of patience, Susanna said, "If you are on fire, sir, then you are in need of a dousing." So saying, she poured the contents of the pail over his head and rushed into the hall.

There she ran headlong into Edward, who had come to the vicarage to see how she did. From the look on her face, he knew at once that she did not do very well.

"Good Lord, Susanna, you aren't in another scrape, are you?"

"Yes, I'm afraid I am." She was breathing hard.

"What happened?" he asked.

Before she could answer, Wilfred stormed into the hall, hissing, "Douse me, will you? You'll be in the workhouse by tonight."

He stopped short when he spied Edward, who burst out laughing at the sight of the young curate's soaked head. Hearing that laughter, Wilfred seethed.

Edward said helpfully, "You are dripping on the floor, sir."

"She did it," Wilfred said, gesturing at Susanna and making her shrink away. Seeing her shiver, Edward put his arm around her shoulder. "She appears to be terrified of you. What did you do to her?"

"*She's* terrified?" Wilfred shrieked. "I'm the one soaked to the skin. I'm the one whose new breeches are ruined. But you will take her part, won't you? Well, my father will take a very different view, I can tell you." His shoes sloshed water as he stalked down the hall and up the stairs.

When he was gone, Edward tried to see Susanna's face but she turned away. She held very still, feeling his arm around her. Respecting her silence, he said nothing. Then, as he continued to hold her, he felt her begin to tremble. Slowly, her tears came, and then sobs. He pulled her to him so that she could cry. "If only I'd been able to get that money for you in London," he said. "Then you would not have to stay here a minute longer."

"Oh, Edward, I wanted so much to put Mama's mind at rest while she lived," she murmured into his lapel. "I wanted her not to worry about me. I miss her so, but I wouldn't have her see me like this for the world. She would be dreadfully disappointed."

"I think she would be smiling at you. She probably is smiling this very moment."

"And Miss Bledsoe—she will be disappointed, too, when she hears that I have been anointing Wilfred Sharpe again."

He smoothed her brilliant curls and nodded. "Miss Bledsoe will say that you ought to have followed her advice to do nothing impolite in answer to rudeness. I'm afraid she will be disappointed that you were so unladylike as to mistake Wilfred for your mop, even though he no doubt deserved it."

Susanna was not at all pleased to have Edward agree with her on the matter of Lucy's disappointment. After all, it was Lucy's advice that had got her into the scrape to begin with. If she had allowed herself to chase her tormentor away at the very start, there would be no scrape to disappoint Lucy. The more she thought about it, the more incensed Susanna grew.

"How dare she be disappointed! It's all her fault!" she cried. "She said I ought to be above rudeness. She said it would not touch me. Well, it did touch me, no matter how far I tried to get above it."

Edward held her away. "I'm glad you did try, and I am very sorry that although you were a lady, Wilfred was not a gentleman. But you cannot blame Lucy for what happened."

"It was she who gave me that absurd piece of advice."

"It is not absurd. I'm sure if Miss Bledsoe had been in a similar situation, she would have found a polite way of getting round Wilfred's misbehaviour. Your methods entertain me hugely, but Miss Bledsoe's are much to be preferred.''

She met his fond smile with a glare. ''I'm glad you find my difficulties entertaining, Edward, but from this day forward, I entertain no one but myself. I've done with being a lady! I've done with ladylike manners!''

''Now that foolish declaration really *will* disappoint Lucy.''

''I've done with Lucy Bledsoe, too!''

Edward stepped back and sought her eyes with his own. ''Please, Susanna,'' he said, ''calm yourself. It's not Miss Bledsoe's fault that you find yourself in another scrape, and you know it. She's been nothing but a friend to you.''

''I don't want her friendship!''

''You are frightened and angry and you miss your mother. You don't mean what you say.''

''I never meant anything more in my life.''

''Susanna, I admire and love Lucy Bledsoe. I mean to marry her some day.''

Susanna felt tears start again. ''Then I am done with you, too,'' she said, and marched with her mop to the kitchen.

FROM THE LETTER she received, Susanna knew that Edward had not told Lucy the cause of their quarrel:

My dear Susanna,
I have scarcely time to write because we are in such a hurry to pack and get away. The doctor says Laurence is very bad again and we must get him to Bath. I know I can rely on your goodness to excuse my not coming to say goodbye. Father calls me to the carriage now, but I cannot end this farewell without say-

ing how truly sorry I am that you and Mr. Farrineau
have quarrelled. Can you not find it in your heart to
forgive him and make it up?

> Believe I am ever your devoted friend,
> Lucy Bledsoe

Susanna read and reread the letter, sighing. She would
have been only too happy to follow Lucy's advice, forgive
Edward, and make it up with him, only he did not come to
see her. She knew it was improper for her to attempt to see
him or write to him, and she felt that the cause of their
quarrel made it imperative that she do what was proper in
this instance. A week passed with no word from Edward,
and then she heard that he had followed the Bledsoes to
Bath.

Once his son had gone, Sir Dalton was at leisure to address the problem that Mr. Sharpe put before him, namely,
what to do about Susanna Marlowe, who had repaid the
vicar's kindness to her by pouring water over poor young
Wilfred's head. Throwing up his hands, Mr. Sharpe did
not know how such uncommonly violent propensities came
to afflict a young woman who had been given every consideration and every opportunity to reform her ways.

After much discussion in the same vein, the gentlemen
concluded that Susanna must go north, where Mr. Sharpe
had a brother in need of a scullery maid. It was hoped that
the cold, bracing air of Scotland, combined with the se-
verity of Rector Josiah Sharpe's character, would improve the young lady and teach her to be grateful.

CHAPTER FOUR

LADY PHILPOTT

SUSANNA WAS NOT as frightened by the prospect of removing to Scotland as Wilfred Sharpe had hoped, and it was no more effective in inducing her to kiss him than any of his threats. She had heard that the country up north was wild and craggy, and her curiosity to see it sustained her as the day of departure approached.

Sir Dalton's plan was to have his carriage take her as far as Worcester, where she would then board the public coach. He knew he ought to take her to her destination. However, the vicar assured him that the ungrateful girl would only take advantage of any consideration, and it would add to her already considerable vanity. The knight was easily persuaded to let her travel by the stage because, truth to tell, he did not like having to use the chaise while his carriage was engaged, and because Edward was in Bath and would not know of the arrangements until it was too late to do anything about them.

The day arrived. Two boxes and a trunk sat in the hall of the vicarage, awaiting Sir Dalton's carriage. Susanna did not wait with them, however. Learning that she need not be ready until noon, she set off on a walk, intending to visit the willow tree she had climbed as a girl. As she walked along the road, admiring the wintercress and Jack by the Hedge, she looked forward to a tender quarter-hour filled with reminiscences, tears and thoughts of Edward.

She was sighing in anticipation of sweet regret when she heard the rumble of a coach behind her. From the sound of it, it appeared to be racing dangerously fast. Moving quickly to the side of the road, she watched the coach hurtle past. It was a handsome equipage, and it bore a crest. More than that, however, she could not see because almost immediately the sight and sound of it vanished. She thought no more about it until she came upon the carriage, stopped on the side of the road with its front wheel in the ditch. The four chestnuts stood peacefully grazing. The coachman lay on the road, unconscious.

Susanna ran to him and knelt by him but was so overcome by the stench of strong drink he gave off that she clapped her hand over her nose. With one hand shielding her from the smell, she employed the other in shaking him and pulling on his arm. After a time, she succeeded in rousing the man sufficiently to induce him to roll out of harm's way.

Exhausted by the effort, she took a breath and turned to examine the coach. She feared that the passengers might be severely shocked or hurt and was on the point of opening the door when suddenly she saw a head appear at the window. It was a gaudy head, heavily powdered and crowned by a purple velvet hat with silver feathers.

"Have you any idea what I paid for this carriage?" the lady asked Susanna. "And now it is destroyed!"

"The wheel may need to be replaced, madam, but I doubt the coach is destroyed," Susanna said.

"What do you know about it? Are you a wheelwright?"

"No, but I have eyes and can see that your wheel is only stuck in the ditch, and that is all."

"I purchased the horses at Tattersall's only last week, paid mighty dearly for them, too. A matched foursome is always very dear. Now, I suppose, you will tell me they are lame and my money has gone out the window."

"I will go and see if they are lame." Susanna went and a few seconds later returned to say, "The horses are well."

"What do you suppose it will cost to have the coach lifted out of the ditch and mended?"

"I don't know," she answered, "but whatever it is, I suppose it must be paid, mustn't it?"

The lady frowned. "You are mighty philosophical for a young lady. I suppose I ought not to be surprised at your insouciance, given the fact that your money is not at stake."

"True, it is not my money. I don't have any money."

"Oh, I am sorry to hear it," the feather-hatted lady said in a gentler tone. "I have been poor myself and I am certain one does much better to be rich. Do you live nearby?"

"I live nowhere, at present. I am going to live in Scotland."

"Just because you have no money? I never heard that they were shipping the poor off to Scotland now. Well, I suppose nobody wants them in the way here. It is so distressing to have to look at them."

"Madam, I think it would be best if you came out of the coach. Should the horses tire of grazing and take it into their heads to move, the coach could fall over and you might be hurt."

The lady looked down and saw that it was a large distance from where she sat to the safety of terra firma. "Just how do you intend to get me out of here, young woman?"

"If you will push open the door, I will jump you down."

"I am a ladyship. I do not go swooping and jumping about. It is not seemly."

At that moment, the horses moved and the coach lurched. It made a creaking noise that frightened the horses, who ran a few yards, dragging it, until a stand of trees brought them to a stop. Susanna ran to the coach to find that the lady had not been hurt; nor had her maid, who whimpered in terror.

The lady permitted Susanna to jump her down, and when she had attained firm ground, she demanded, "Is my hat ruined? I bought it only last week and a pretty penny I paid for it, too."

"The bonnet is very well, madam. But are you all right, and your young woman there?"

The lady pinched her arms and cheeks and those of her lady's maid. "It appears we are still alive."

Looking about her, Susanna sought out a shady spot and spread her shawl on the grass so that the older woman and the maid might sit. "You may sit here, if you like," Susanna invited. "Meanwhile, I will see what I can do for the horses."

With many a sigh at the indignity she was forced to suffer, the lady allowed her maid to help her sit down as gracefully as her plumpness would allow.

After calming the horses, Susanna freed one of the leaders. The three remaining horses she tied to a tree. Then she mounted the bare back of her leader, shouted, "I will bring the wheelwright," and started in the direction of Cheedham.

Mr. Mees, the wheelwright, lost no time in coming to the rescue of the lady, and as soon as he saw the magnificence of her equipage and the crest it bore, he anticipated a good profit. He sent his boy back to town with the cart and the drunken coachman, and when the boy returned, Susanna persuaded the wheelwright to delay his repairs in order to drive the lady to some safe place.

"Her ladyship ought not to be forced to wait hours in the road until her coach is fixed," Susanna pointed out.

The wheelwright, flashing an amiable, toothless smile, heartily agreed.

"Well, my man, as long as you are swoofing up and down the road, you might as well take me to Langfield," said the lady. "That is where I was bound for to begin with. Is it far?"

"Langfield?" Susanna repeated.

"Yes, indeed, and you will come with us, if you please."

"Oh, no, Sir Dalton would not be at all glad to see me."

"He won't be glad to see me either, but I do not pay him any mind. I should never visit anybody if I paid them any mind."

"But you see, I am expected at the vicarage soon. Sir Dalton's carriage will be coming for me. It will take me to Worcester, where I am to meet the stagecoach. I believe I mentioned that I am going to Scotland."

"Scotland will just have to wait," said her ladyship, allowing Mr. Mees to hand her into his cart. Then the wheelwright looked at Susanna, his arm extended, ready to hand her up.

For an instant, she hesitated, unsure of what she ought to do. Was it right, she asked herself, to defy Sir Dalton and Mr. Sharpe on the very last day and in the very last hour of her residence in Cheedham?

"Come along," the lady said, "and tomorrow I will buy you a new shawl. Yours has been ruined in my service and I shall not fail to show my gratitude. It was not an expensive shawl, to be sure, and may be easily replaced at little cost."

Susanna still hung back.

"My dear girl," said her ladyship in a gentle voice, "you have gone to all the trouble of saving my life. The least you can do is see that it is a happy life. Will you do me the kindness of obliging me in this?'' And here she smiled.

It had been a very long time since anyone had spoken gently to Susanna. The last time—she remembered it down to the smallest detail—had been when Edward had found her in the vicarage, just before they had quarrelled. Such gentleness was irresistable. Therefore, Susanna took the wheelwright's hand, stepped into the cart and took her place by the lady's side.

SIR DALTON WAS SO SHOCKED to see her ladyship that he did not notice her companion.

''Where is my sister-in-law?'' the lady asked, not waiting to be invited to sit, but sweeping to one of the sofas and spreading herself across its cushion. Susanna hovered near a bust of a dead Greek, wondering if she should stay or tiptoe out the door.

Sir Dalton replied, ''I have sent the servant for Lady Farrineau. But she said not a word to me about your visit. I am very surprised to see you.''

''I never told her I meant to visit, and, in fact, I only meant to overnight with you as I am on the road south. I see no need to go to the expense of putting up at an inn when I have relations only a few miles out of the way. But now my carriage has broken down, and I suppose I shall be forced to visit you.''

The knight declared, ''I shall have my people assist with the repairs.''

''Thank you, Dalty. You want me to be gone as quickly as I can, and I am happy to oblige.''

Suddenly Sir Dalton noticed Susanna. ''Why are you here, Miss Marlowe? You are supposed to be at the vicarage.''

"I brought her here," said the lady. "She saved my life."

He regarded Susanna steadily. His gaze was expressive of many emotions, none of which included gratitude for the rescue of his relation. "This is most inconvenient," he said. "I sent my coach to the vicarage not ten minutes ago."

Susanna would have apologized, but Lady Philpott demanded to know, "What is this nonsense about your sending her to Scotland, Dalty? Why should you deprive England of a brave and useful young woman? Heaven knows, we have enough of the other sort."

"The girl has been troublesome and a burden on the village. We have to do something with her."

At this juncture, Lady Farrineau appeared. She wore the smile she had affixed to her lips when the butler had warned her who was within.

"Sally, what do you know about this Scotland business?" Lady Philpott demanded. "It seems a shame to banish a young woman who speaks as well as this one does and is so evidently educated, intelligent and sensible. I daresay she would also be pretty if she used a little rouge."

"I do not interfere in my husband's business," Lady Farrineau replied.

"How very odd. I always interfered in your brother's business. I believe he bore up very well."

"Each gentleman is different, to be sure. Sir Dalton and Edward take care of their business and I take care of mine. In contrast, I recall my brother's saying that he had particularly looked for a wife who would be active in all his affairs."

"Did he say that?" Lady Philpott exclaimed. "Dear man. I thought he married me to disoblige his family. I was awfully poor, you know, and my education was quite pitiful. And he did disoblige everyone by marrying me.''

''He did indeed,'' said Sir Dalton.

''Still I don't see why you have to send this charming young creature away. Is there no one who wants her?''

''No one, more's the pity,'' said Lady Farrineau.

''Surely there is an elderly gentleman, a rich one, a widower who would like a bright and cheerful companion for his waning days and would marry Miss Marlowe in order to get one.''

Susanna blanched as she heard this suggestion.

Sir Dalton came to her rescue, however, by declaring there was no one who wanted her for a week, let alone the rest of his waning days. ''And besides, who would marry a beggar?'' he asked.

''Your wife's brother married one, didn't he?'' Lady Philpott pointed out, ''and I made him prodigiously happy, too.''

Sir Dalton threw up his hands. His wife, attempting to placate both her husband and her sister-in-law, asked her guest if she wished to take tea now.

''Miss Marlowe will have tea with us,'' stated Lady Philpott.

Sir Dalton glared at his guest. ''I hope that you do not take up this young woman's cause solely in order to vex me. I assure you, I have thought long and hard on her situation and believe Scotland will answer her difficulty.''

Lady Philpott smiled. ''I dearly love to vex you, Dalty, but I have no intention of doing so in this instance.'' Here she marched to Susanna, tucked her small hand in her own very large one and brought her forward. ''Since no one in the country has the wit to keep her, I shall keep her myself. She will stay here with me as your guest until my carriage is repaired, and then I shall take her with me as my travelling companion."

Lady Farrineau bit her lip. She had spoken the truth when she'd said she did not interfere in her husband's business. Still, it seemed to her that in Edward's absence, someone had to speak on Susanna's behalf. Lady Philpott was whimsical and impulsive. There was no guarantee that she would not tire of Susanna and leave her stranded. Had Edward been there, he would not have hesitated for a moment to speak. Therefore, as his mother, it behooved Lady Farrineau to say a word.

Approaching Susanna, she asked, "Tell us, Miss Marlowe, what do you wish to do? You have a choice before you, and you need not go with Lady Philpott unless you want to."

Susanna looked from one face to the other. If she had a real choice, she would have elected to stay in Cheedham, where she knew everyone and was known by everyone. Surely Edward would not be gone from home forever, and it was the greatest wish of her heart to be in Cheedham when he returned. But as that was not one of her alternatives, she hardly knew what to say.

"Miss Marlowe," said Lady Farrineau carefully, "do you understand the opportunity that lies before you? In Scotland you will be able to begin afresh. Whatever may have appeared in the past to tarnish your reputation or bring you misfortune may be put behind you there. At the rectory of Mr. Sharpe's brother, you may enjoy the contemplative sort of life conducive to the reform of manners and morals. On the other side, you have an invitation— such as it is—to go and live with Lady Philpott, whom you met scarcely a few hours ago, and who has not said how long she means to keep you or what she intends to do for you. She has not even said where she means to take you."

Lady Philpott shook her powdered curls, letting her hat feathers bounce prettily. "You talk as though I swoofed about here and there with no purpose and no forethought," she said lightly. "I assure you, I do no such thing." Turning to Susanna, she asked, "Do you not wish to come with me?"

"But where would you take me?" Susanna asked.

Her ladyship replied, "Well, I have let a house in Bath and am on my way there now. My dear, do you think you would like to go to Bath?"

THEY ENTERED THE CITY by crossing the Avon at the Old Bridge and were driven up Stall Street to the White Hart, where they were to stay a day or two before taking up residence. It was a mild, drizzly day that cast a delicate haze over the city. From the carriage window, Susanna saw crescents of honey-coloured houses prettily lined among billowy trees of green. Lady Philpott craned her neck to see the sights. She had never been to Bath—her husband had abhorred watering places—but she had heard that the shopping there was unequalled. She meant to visit all the shops and fit out her young companion as prettily as was consistent with careful economy.

When they removed to Sydney Place, Lady Philpott declared it to be a disappointing location, complaining, "It is far from the shopping. What was my agent thinking of when he set us up in such an outlying street? Why, it is positively rural."

Susanna explored the street on foot the next day and quickly discovered the delights of their situation. Across from the house lay the Sydney Gardens, where she and her hostess could enjoy the public breakfasts in fine weather. Readily accessible, too, was Great Pulteney Street, a fashionable centre at the end of which lay a bridge into the city.

And hard by the house was a canal with a path alongside it.

As she walked, Susanna wondered how soon she would see Edward. When she did see him, what would she say? What would he say? Would he be willing to speak to her at all?

She had much time to ponder these questions because until her clothes could be readied and she might be considered fit to be seen, her ladyship left her at the house and went about the town alone. This Lady Philpott found to be unsatisfactory, for one was required to walk everywhere, owing to the steepness of the streets, and one could not very well walk by oneself. It was the work of a single day to inscribe their names in the subscription books at the assembly rooms, to be greeted by Mr. King, and to peruse the newspaper to find out the names of the new arrivals. After that, there was nothing to do. She detested shopping by herself. "Everything is so very dear nowadays; one needs someone to complain to, even if one must end by paying the price."

Most disappointing of all was the discovery that her nephew Edward was not to be found. When she sent a note to his lodgings, she was told that he had gone away on business. Susanna would have suggested that a note be sent to the Bledsoes, for she was certain Lady Philpott would enjoy their society, especially the conversation and elegance of Miss Lucy, but she did not know their direction.

Meanwhile, Susanna was content to entertain herself with walks. There was much to see along the canal—an orange-beaked coot, a nest of birds, small pleasure boats carrying finely dressed ladies and gentlemen, the view of a church tower.

Lady Philpott protested against this form of amusement. "I do not know how you can walk so long and so far," she said. "I haven't any patience with nature. One quickly becomes bored, and then what is one to do? The rest of the time must be spent in talking endlessly about what one glanced at for scarcely a second. One is obliged to appear nobly uplifted by the sight. I much prefer looking in shops."

When the dressmaker had sewn enough dresses, her ladyship determined to take Susanna out. First, there were walks around the city. Bath was not so fashionable a spa as it used to be, Lady Philpott had learned; nevertheless, one had to exert oneself to be seen everywhere. Each day they spent considerable time being elbowed by the crowd at the Pump Room, where Susanna found the orchestra soothing and the waters vile. Next door to the Pump Room, Susanna was introduced to the Meyler & Sons library. Finally, they attended a gala at the Sydney Gardens, which provided a very fine display of illuminated waterfalls.

One afternoon in Milsom Street, while the ladies conjectured as to the price of some *coquelicot* ribbons in a shop window, her ladyship was greeted by a young gentleman. Soon Susanna was introduced to Lord Blessington, who eyed her appearance minutely, approved its fashion and taste and permitted himself to ask, "Will you attend the assembly rooms tonight, Miss Marlowe?"

Susanna turned a questioning face to her hostess.

"I suppose we might do so," replied her ladyship, "if you will be so kind as to take us, Blessington."

The young man thought a moment. "I had an idea of taking Miss Orton, but as you have asked and she hasn't, I suppose I may wait and see her there. I shall ask her to dance, after I have danced with Miss Murchen-Hill."

"And Miss Marlowe," said Lady Philpott slyly.

"Oh, yes," said the gentleman. He glanced at Susanna's green spencer and muslin skirt. "I shall be honoured to dance with Miss Marlowe, too."

Susanna nodded and turned to look at the ribbons again.

In another moment, the young man took his leave, promising to procure the tickets for the assembly and to call for them before nine.

"My dear girl," Lady Philpott said in Susanna's ear "I wish you had been more lively with Lord Blessington. He is very rich and was much taken with you, I fancy."

"I hope I was not impolite," Susanna replied. "Of late, I try to say as little as I can."

"I have noticed you are uncommonly quiet for a girl. I thought it was just your odd way, but now you say you keep mum on purpose?"

"I study to be quiet, your ladyship, for I have too often in the past spoken only to give offence."

"A certain tranquillity is not a bad thing. The gentlemen like it, for they prefer to do the talking themselves. But you must say something from time to time, my dear, if only to assure them that you are still awake. You are intelligent and you speak very well when you've a mind to, but in the company of young men, you must bestir yourself to put forward topics of discussion."

"I hardly know what to say, and I'm afraid of saying the wrong thing."

"Fiddle! All you need do is to ask Lord Blessington whether he is pleased with Bath and whether he has a large acquaintance here. I assure you, you will not be required to say anything else, for, in the main, gentlemen love to talk and only want an opening. After that, you should strive to seem wildly interested in whatever interests them."

"Why?"

"Why?" repeated her ladyship. "You ask why?"

"Yes, why?"

"Well, because that is how it is done."

"How what is done?"

"How a young woman gets a husband."

Susanna was stopped. "I am amazed, my lady. Are you thinking I am going to be married?"

"Of course I am thinking it. I am thinking nothing else of late. How else are you to live? You surely do not expect me to have the expense of supporting you the rest of my days."

Susanna lowered her eyes. "No, certainly not."

"Not that I shouldn't like to have your companionship always, dear girl. You really are very convenient and don't go swoofing about or rattling on like so many girls. But I do not engage to keep you in clothing for very much longer. Young ladies are so awfully expensive."

Susanna frowned. "Lady Philpott, are you thinking of my marrying Lord Blessington?"

"He is certainly eligible."

"But surely he would not marry me. You have heard the story of my father's scandalous flight from England. You know all about my difficulties in Cheedham. It is impossible that his lordship would align himself to a woman with so little to recommend her in the way of reputation and worldly advantages."

"He must not hear a word regarding your father or your past career. Secrecy is of the utmost importance."

Susanna turned a sad smile on her benefactress. "Then I'm afraid I shall be forced to tell him, for I will not lie."

Lady Philpott smiled archly at Susanna. "You have my permission to tell him anything you like—after he is in love with you and the engagement is formed. Now, what do you say to those ribbons? They will look perfect on your new bonnet, will they not? I think we must go in and inquire about them, and if they are not absolutely, outrageously dear, you shall have them.''

THE ENTRANCE to the Upper Rooms was crowded with chairs, passengers and servants, so that there was a delay in gaining admission to the hall. Once inside, Lord Blessington cursed their ill luck at being kept waiting so long. "We have missed the before tea," he lamented. "There are very good dances at the before tea, and I meant to ask Miss DuMar for a set."

As he looked around for the young lady in question, Susanna looked about her, too, and wondered how any one could recognize any one else in such a crowd. She had no time to wonder, however, for his lordship exhorted them to follow him through the crowd. He found them each a place before one of the fires in the Octagon Room. There they stood, each with her cup of tea, while Lord Blessington went in search of Miss DuMar. His departure afforded Susanna the opportunity of observing the fashionable men and women and listening to Lady Philpott's speculation as to how much their attire must have impoverished them.

Lord Blessington returned to report that he had failed to locate Miss DuMar and was in dread of her taking his neglect as a slight. "We might as well go into the assembly room and look for her there," he said. "If she is not there, perhaps Miss Murchen-Hill will wish to dance."

Thereupon, they set down their cups and were led into the room where the dancing was going forward. After acknowledging the gracious welcome of the Master of Ceremonies, they were permitted to take a place by the chairs directly across from the musicians' gallery. From this vantage point, they could see one of the entrances to the room, and Susanna found her eyes turned on these doors more and more often, as though she expected to see Edward walk through them at the next moment.

"I see Miss DuMar!" Lord Blessington announced triumphantly. "There she is." Susanna followed him with her eyes as he made his way across the room, dodging the dancers and the talkers, but he was soon lost to view. A moment later, he surprised her by popping up again. "Miss DuMar is engaged the whole evening!" he exclaimed. "I am too late. Her card is already full."

"In that case," said Lady Philpott, "you have my permission to ask Miss Marlowe to dance."

Lord Blessington regarded Susanna as though she had previously been invisible and had only now been made manifest. "Would you do me the honour?" he asked cordially.

Lady Philpott winked and nodded to her protégée to indicate encouragement, and so Susanna set her hand on his lordship's arm and was led forward into the set. Happily the *boulanger* was the dance, and so intricate did the gentleman find the steps that he had little time for conversation. The most he could do was to hope aloud that Miss Murchen-Hill would soon show herself.

As the dance ended and they were leaving the floor, his lordship stood stock-still and exclaimed, "By Jove, look who has come in. It is Miss Hargreaves!"

Susanna looked where he pointed and saw Edward Farrineau looking at her. He did not move or attempt to come forward. It seemed to her, from the steadiness of his gaze, that he must have been looking at her for some time. At first, she suspected that he did not recognize her. But, even though he was at some distance, she discerned a starkness in his expression that said he knew exactly who she was.

Because the sudden sight of him took her by surprise, she did not think to smile. Then a line of dancers came between them; she could not see him any longer; and it was too late to smile.

CHAPTER FIVE

TAKING THE CURE

"MISS MARLOWE," said a voice behind her.

Before Susanna turned, she knew she would see him, and when she did turn and her eyes met his, she found she could not speak. She would have liked to pronounce his name and to say how sorry she was for all she had done to drive him off, but she could not do so in the presence of Lord Blessington. The last thing she wished to do was to offend Edward with another impulsive outburst.

"How do you do, Farrineau?" said Lord Blessington, greeting Edward familiarly. "You know Miss Marlowe?"

Edward did not look at Blessington but kept his eyes on Susanna. "We've known each other nearly all our lives," he said.

At that moment, Lady Philpott spied her nephew with Susanna and, crying out his name, joined him at once. Blessington took advantage of her approach to seek out Miss DuMar.

"Edward, what did you mean by leaving Bath just when I arrived?" demanded his aunt. "It looked as if you wished to avoid me."

Taking his eyes from Susanna, he answered, "I did not know I would have the honour of seeing you here, Aunt. You did not let me know you were coming. And I had business at Langfield."

"Langfield? Why, we've just come from there."

He glanced briefly at Susanna before saying, "Yes, so I understand."

"I have no opinion of all this swoofing about—first to Bath, then to Cheedham, then to Bath again. It makes you out to be restless and inconstant."

"I had received a letter saying that Miss Marlowe was shortly to be banished to Scotland. Naturally I wasted no time in returning home."

Susanna bowed her head.

"Much good you would have done. So far as I can tell, they none of them have her interest at heart, and I daresay if you had tried to talk them out of Scotland, they would not have heard a word you said. It's a good thing my carriage stuck in the ditch. Otherwise, the poor child might be eating haggis even now." Here the lady shuddered violently.

Edward looked grave and said nothing.

"Well," said Lady Philpott with a sigh, "it has all turned out happily and I mean to see she is provided for." With her black lace fan, she tapped her nephew on the arm and said, "My dear boy, ask her to dance. And stop looking so gloomy. I daresay you will frown the poor girl out of her wits."

He turned to Susanna with a bow and invited her to dance. Nodding, she accepted, and they went down to join the set.

They executed a number of slow turns and graceful circles, during which Edward fixed his eyes on her. So heavy was his expression that Susanna began to fear he was still angry at her. His manner towards her had been stiff and cold, and his unwavering gravity gave every indication that his anger had not softened. She began to think he would never forgive her.

The pain this realization caused was acute, the more so because it resurrected losses of recent years—the flight of her father and the death of her mother. If the dance had not required Edward to take her hand at that moment and turn her inside the circle, she might not have been able to withstand the force of these recollections.

Closing her eyes for a moment, she took a solemn vow never to quarrel with him again. It did not matter how many utterances she had to bury, how many impulses she had to suppress. She would not, she could not, sustain another loss. Nothing would be worse than knowing that Edward was lost to her forever.

The dance obliged them to lock arms, and Edward took the opportunity of saying, "Susanna, I will never leave you in that way again. If I had stayed, they would never have dared to mention Scotland. I should have prevented them. I blame myself for what happened. I thank God for Lady Philpott."

When she looked at him, she found his expression full of warmth. "It is not your fault you went to Bath," she said earnestly. "I foolishly drove you off. I won't do it again."

He nodded almost bitterly. "It's true, you won't drive me off again, because I won't be driven off. Even if you beg me to leave you, I won't do it."

She smiled. "In that case, I shall not bother to beg you."

He studied her, then laughed. "Then I need not feel sorry for you any longer. I see you are well enough to tease me."

"Yes, I am very well now."

"You look very well. I failed to recognize you at first. You are not the young girl I knew in Cheedham."

"Lady Philpott dresses me up, puts combs in my hair and in general looks after me."

"I mean to look after you, too. There will be no more Scotlands, I can promise you that."

"Edward, while we are in a vowing and promising frame of mind, I want to tell you this: I know I was very wrong to speak as I did of Miss Bledsoe."

He smiled at her. "That is what I wanted to hear more than anything in the world. It means a great deal to me to know that you will get on with her. I want you to like her. I've asked her to marry me."

"Oh."

"And the next time I ask her, I fully intend to make her accept me."

"Do you mean she has refused you?"

"Mind your steps, Susanna. You nearly kicked that poor fellow. Yes, she refused me."

"But that is impossible."

He laughed again. "Only you, Susanna, could fail to believe that I could be refused, and I am flattered. But you are too partial and, consequently, blind to my faults."

"Did Miss Bledsoe give you any reason for her refusal?"

"She wishes to know my character. She is too wise to engage herself to one whose past career has been as unsteady as mine."

"Unsteady! But you have loved her forever. It was ages ago, at Edenhurst, that you introduced her to me as the young lady you meant to marry. I remember it as though it were yesterday."

"By all means, defend me. But if you keep on this way, I shall have to add conceit to my other failings."

Susanna would have protested further but she caught herself in time. She had vowed not to say a word against Miss Bledsoe and she meant to keep that vow, especially now, when she saw that to keep quiet was very much in her own interest.

THE BLEDSOES were immediately introduced to Lady Philpott, and Lucy's smile of pleasure at the sight of Susanna showed that the warm greeting was sincere. Her ladyship was soon engaged in conversation with Mr. Bledsoe, with whom she got on very well, for while the widow estimated the cost of each item of apparel anyone wore, the widower estimated the fortune of the wearer.

Edward asked Lucy to dance, leaving Susanna and Laurence Bledsoe to entertain one another. The young man took a moment to admire his companion's profile as she watched her two friends dance the reel. Then he said, "You will excuse my not asking you to dance, I hope. I have had my two dances, and the doctor forbids me any more."

Susanna looked at him. "You are not well, Mr. Bledsoe?"

He smiled. "That is why I've come to Bath."

"I'd forgotten that there are those who come here for their health. I had begun to think everyone came to shop and to meet their acquaintance under the most crowded conditions."

"My purpose in coming is to sip the foul-tasting waters."

"Lady Philpott says they make her ill."

"I believe the waters are intended to cure illness, not cause it. But perhaps her ladyship has confused the two. Tomorrow I am to drink at the Hetling Pump. If the odour does not overcome me altogether, I may even be cured."

"Would you prefer to sit? Perhaps you are tired."

When they sat, Laurence said, "I have long been wanting to apologize to you. I wished to visit after your mother died. She was kind to me once when I was ill."

Susanna lowered her eyes.

"Do you recall accompanying her on a visit to our house? I remember she had the servant bring us a bushel of apples from your orchard at Edenhurst, and while she came inside and showed Lucy how to bake one for me, you stood guard over the bushel basket in the garden."

"I have a feeling, sir, that you are about to tell me a tale of mischief. In those days, I did little else but fall into it."

"Well, there was mischief, but the blame was not yours."

She looked at him with curiosity and he smiled as he went on. "Wilfred Sharpe happened along. I'm afraid that young man is very much the bully, for all he is the vicar's son. I saw him say something to you—I could not hear what it was—and when you answered, he set up a howl. He stamped his foot, and then began hurling all your mother's apples into the daisies. At first you tried to retrieve the apples, but when you saw that it availed you nothing, you jumped onto his back and grasped his nose until he cried, 'Surrender!' I was mighty pleased when I heard some years later that it was owing to your good offices that the town calls him Lily-livered Willy."

She sighed. "Oh, I wish I had remembered that tale. I should have looked back on it with pleasure these many years."

The young man leaned towards her. "I have never heard a young lady express herself as you do."

She blushed. "I am endeavouring to overcome that defect in my manners, sir. I apologize if I offended you."

"Oh, no, I like it. It is highly interesting."

She regarded him with amazement, and recalling one or two instructions Lady Philpott had whispered in her ear on their way out the door that evening, she took a breath and asked, "Are you pleased with Bath?"

He talked for some minutes on the amusements the city afforded and the attractions of the surrounding country.

Susanna was delighted to see that her ladyship's advice could be so easily and so successfully applied. Therefore, she asked, "Have you a large acquaintance in Bath?"

There now followed a description of the people they had known for years past and those whom they had been so fortunate as to meet for the first time that season. He concluded his speech by asking, "Why do you smile like that?"

"I thought I did very well, don't you?" Susanna asked. "I mean, I asked you exactly what I ought to have asked and you answered me at some length."

Maintaining a serious expression, he nodded. "We both did rather well. I daresay we might do it again sometime."

He engaged to call on her soon, and Susanna congratulated herself on having accomplished a great deal in the past hours, for not only had she managed to converse sensibly with a young gentleman, but she had reconciled with Edward and had behaved herself with prodigious propriety.

EDWARD CALLED at Sydney Place the next day and was soon followed by the Bledsoes. Lord Blessington called late but was forced to be content with leaving his card, for the others had gone out. With all of them snug in Lady Philpott's large curricle, they went on a drive to Landsdown Hill.

It was a fine day, and although Lady Philpott did not in general approve of excursions whose object was the viewing of nature, the company was so jolly that she was even induced to leave her carriage and walk to where she might admire a pretty view of the city. That bit of a walk was sufficient exercise for the day, she declared, so that when the others suggested a walk to the hilltop, she preferred to wait in the carriage. Because Laurence Bledsoe was still tired from the efforts of the previous night, he cheerfully volunteered to keep Lady Philpott company.

The four walkers set off across a tiny bridge and then along a steep path. It was not long before Mr. Bledsoe and Edward outstripped the two young ladies, who put up their parasols and walked for some time in silence. The rigours of climbing gave them an excuse for silence. But when the path grew gentler, their pace eased and Lucy said, "I have been thinking about your situation ever since I learned you were to go to Scotland, and I cannot help wondering what you will do."

Susanna turned to her. "I wonder myself."

"It is very good of Lady Philpott to take you under her wing, but what does she propose to do for you? It is all so vague, and I am afraid for you. Suppose she quarrels with you, or wearies of you? What will become of you then?"

"Her ladyship thinks I ought to find a husband to assume the expense of keeping me, which occasionally she finds irksome."

Lucy bit her lip. "Do you wish to marry?"

"I would not say that I wish it, precisely," Susanna said, "but I believe it would answer, don't you? When you think about it, I am not fit for anything else. I am too well educated to be very good at scullery work or dressmaking. No one in Cheedham will recommend me as a governess. I might make a career as a travelling companion and when Lady Philpott sends me away, simply find another to take me on, but there is not much security in that, I'm afraid.

Against these alternatives, marriage seems to offer the least difficulty.''

They resumed walking.

Lucy said, ''You would not say that about marriage if you knew anything about the misery of an unsuitable one. I saw many in town during my lengthy stay, and I can tell you, I shall take every precaution to avoid such a union myself.''

''It is true I have neither experienced nor observed an unsuitable marriage,'' Susanna replied. ''But I have worked in Mr. Sharpe's scullery, I have gone to bed at night with my stomach yawning in hunger, and I have heard Lady Philpott's distress at every bill she incurs on my behalf. Marriage would at least give me a home of my own, a certain independence and the dignity of being someone's wife.''

Lucy shook her head ruefully. ''Whom does her ladyship wish you to marry?''

''She has high hopes for Lord Blessington, it seems. He, however, does not notice me. I'm afraid I don't have the knack of being noticed by gentlemen.''

''You must not use Lord Blessington as your touchstone. You are very noticeable and he is a perfect dolt. You will kindly oblige me by not marrying him.''

Susanna sighed. She sometimes wished that Lucy did not cherish such generous sentiments towards her, for she could not return them in full. There must always be some reservation, some reminder of Edward, some little jealousy. ''Why do you not marry?'' Susanna asked. ''Why do you not marry Mr. Farrineau?''

Lucy smiled. ''He told you that he asked me?''

''Yes, and that you refused. I don't understand it.''

''He may change his mind and wish to marry someone else.''

"That is not very likely. He is in love with you."

"But I do not know whether I am in love with him. I have the highest regard for him, but I cannot call it love."

"What more do you require?"

"I hardly know myself, but perhaps I will know my feelings better when I know more of his character."

"You amaze me."

"Do I? Is it so impossible for you to imagine that anyone can withstand the charms of Mr. Farrineau?"

"It amazes me to see you so rational in a situation where my sensibilities would rule me utterly. Mr. Farrineau is exceedingly handsome and has a comfortable income. In time, he will be rich. His name is one of the most respected in England, and his heart one of the gentlest. He is interesting, amusing and amiable. To be adored by such a man is what every woman wishes—to be looked at as he looks at you, to be valued as he values you. Few women have the power to refuse such a man."

"You think I am insensible and hard."

"No, I think you are strong. I could not be so strong."

Lucy stole a glimpse at her companion and frowned. "I wonder if you can view the matter as I do, without any interferences from your long-standing loyalty and friendship to Mr. Farrineau. The only man I can love is a man of character, and I have some reason to doubt Mr. Farrineau's character. He knew you were in a desperate situation at the vicarage, and yet he left you to come here. He knew it was wrong; he said as much to me. But he did it, anyway. If not for Lady Philpott, his conscience would give him no rest now."

"But I insulted him. I told him I wanted none of him."

"He did not do what a gentleman ought to have done. It shows a want of temper. I cannot love a man who shows a tendency toward pique, one which is capable of making him selfish and thoughtless of what a gentleman owes to others. When I marry, it will be to a man who is capable of setting aside his own pride for the sake of principle.''

Susanna was moved to defend Edward but was saved the trouble by Lucy, who said, ''Let me assure you that I have endeavoured to overlook this most recent lapse. Your friendship with him is of such a nature as to excuse any response that is more feeling than it is polite. Naturally, where you are concerned, his emotions may be expected to overcome him. I have made allowances as best I can. Besides, if you are able to forgive him, how can I do less?''

''You must not judge him on that basis alone. Remember that Mr. Farrineau gave my mother Larkwhistle Cottage. His generosity meant that she did not have to die on the street or in the workhouse. And I ask you to look at what happened only last week. When he heard of my distress—of my imminent banishment—he went at once to Langfield. He was ready to do battle against the vicar—against his own father—against the whole county if need be, on my behalf. Is that not character, Lucy?''

''I suppose it is.''

''He has told me he means to look after me. He has promised we will never quarrel again, and even if we do, he will not let it drive him off again. I believe he means every word of it.''

Lucy stopped to inspect a row of wildflowers, while Susanna wondered how she had contrived to place herself in the position of pleading Edward's cause with Lucy. She resolved to remain mum henceforth, and there was a long silence until the gentlemen appeared on the path. Mr. Bledsoe asked if the ladies were tired; Edward asked if they cared to turn back now.

The pace the four of them set was leisurely. The gentlemen had had their fill of outwalking each other and the ladies looked forward to inconsequential conversation. Lucy and Edward soon fell behind the other two, talking in voices too low to be heard.

Mr. Bledsoe and Susanna walked without saying a word. It was clear from the gentleman's expression that he was not pleased at the thought that someone might see him with so disgraceful a companion as Henry Marlowe's daughter. Susanna did not catch his expression, however, and therefore paid it no heed. Her thoughts dwelt on the necessity of practising her manners and making herself agreeable.

"Are you pleased with Bath?" she asked him.

At first he looked alarmed. Then he persuaded himself to answer, which he did for many minutes, detailing the same facts that Laurence Bledsoe had given her the previous evening but with the embellishment of a great many opinions.

By the time he had finished speaking, they were nearly halfway down the hill, and Susanna asked, "Do you have a large acquaintance in Bath?"

This question inspired a speech lasting many minutes, during which time Susanna learned all about the richest residents in the city and the extent of their debts and fortunes.

He had just concluded when Lucy and Edward came up. The four walked together until the path narrowed, and then a slight rearrangement took place. Mr. Bledsoe moved to his daughter to whisper in her ear that the Marlowe girl was not nearly so bad as he had remembered and that she had surprised him by making very lively and intelligent conversation. Lucy put her arm in his, and thus Edward and Susanna were left to stroll together.

Edward permitted Lucy and her father to walk on ahead, and when they had gone far enough to give him some privacy, he said to Susanna, "Lucy tells me you are to be married. Is it true? Is that what my aunt has in view?"

"Yes, I think it is."

"I shall speak to her. She will not press you once I've spoken to her. The idea of your marrying—it's absurd."

"Your aunt was in a situation very similar to mine once, and she married her way out of it. It is not at all absurd for her to have the same ambition for me."

"Is that what you want?"

"What else is there for me to do?"

"There must be something. It cannot be impossible for a respectable woman to live respectably without being either a governess or a wife."

"I'm afraid it is impossible, unless she has nieces or nephews, in which case she is permitted to be a maiden aunt."

"I am not speaking in the abstract, Susanna. I am speaking of you, and I don't think you ought to be married."

"Well, then, do you know of anyone who is advertising for a governess and will not give me my notice if I tell his children my true opinion of Julius Caesar?"

"Will you be serious, Susanna. We are not talking about an adventure or a lark. Marriage is a very serious business."

"Yes, it is. Miss Bledsoe has been telling me just how serious it is, and I see now what I did not see before, that a young lady must think very carefully about her future."

"Did Miss Bledsoe say that? I suppose she was speaking of me." He looked troubled when he said it.

"Miss Bledsoe is everything that is admirable in a woman. No wonder you are in love with her, Edward."

"I venture to say Miss Bledsoe doesn't think you ought to marry your way out of your situation. She will agree with me in thinking it absurd."

"She did not like the idea, but I believe she saw the necessity of it."

"Then I shall speak to her. I shall speak to Lady Philpott, as well. I shall speak to them both, and they shall know my view of your marrying."

Susanna was on the point of begging him not to say anything, but she refrained. It occurred to her that she was headed for another quarrel with Edward, and she wanted to avoid it at any cost. It was unlike her to avoid a quarrel, unlike her to think before speaking her thoughts, but she made the effort in this instance. At first, she was uncomfortable in the struggle to hold her tongue; then she grew easier as it struck her that it was most pleasant to have Edward object to her being married.

THE CURRICLE dropped Mr. Bledsoe and his son at their lodgings in Marlborough Buildings. Mr. Laurence was obliged to prepare for his pilgrimage to the Helting Pump and his father had to accompany him. Lucy rode to Sydney Place with the others, and when they were all seated inside the house, sipping tea and enjoying the fine view of the gardens across the way, Edward got up from his chair and paced the room. Miss Bledsoe was equally preoccupied.

Only Lady Philpott spoke her thoughts aloud. The view from the window was pretty enough if one liked flowers and grass, but one never saw one's acquaintance strolling along. There was never an opportunity to open the window, shout to a familiar face and receive or give an invitation. She ought to have taken a house nearer the shops, where there was always activity aplenty and the rents were not nearly so high.

Susanna observed it all and sighed. She blamed herself for the silent preoccupation of her two friends. It was all this talk of her marrying that had distressed them. She dreaded to think what might follow from it.

To dispel the general gloom, she said, "Lady Philpott, I have done very ill to two of the best people of the world. I have set them to worrying and now must ask your advice on undoing the harm I have done."

Edward and Lucy glanced up at her, then at each other. Lady Philpott tore her eyes from the hopeless street and asked what on earth Susanna had done. "My dear, you have not gone and thrown a pail of water on anyone as you did in Cheedham, have you? I'm afraid we would not be received well if it got out that you gave a gentleman a dousing. They have the baths here for that."

"I behaved myself as well as I could and did not give anyone a dousing. But I did speak of marriage."

"Whose marriage?" asked her ladyship.

"Mine. The one that is to rescue me from my present straits."

"Oh, yes. Well, I think we ought to be able to find someone for you by the end of the season. It would certainly forward things, however, if Miss Bledsoe and my nephew would help."

Edward whipped round. "I have no intention of helping in any such scheme. It's cruel. It's ludicrous."

Lucy stood up and said, "I don't understand you. Why is it permissable for me to be married but not Miss Marlowe? I am sure she will make an excellent wife, as good or better than myself."

Something in her tone pained him. He was shocked, agitated.

"Why don't you answer me?" Lucy demanded.

"I don't know what to say. I did not mean to imply anything against Susanna. I'm sure she would make a fine wife."

"But you won't hear of her marrying. Why not?"

He collected himself enough to reply, "It's not that I won't hear of her marrying. I merely don't want to see her do anything desperate, or foolish or ill-judged. I want her to be happy."

Lady Philpott rose from the window seat then to nod her agreement. "Yes, our dear Miss Marlowe must be happy. We can't have her marrying just anybody. She is a brave and intelligent young woman, and she can be quite charming when she exerts herself to speak."

Lucy and Edward still looked at each other as if they had just had their first quarrel. Indeed, Susanna guessed that they had never so much as disagreed before now. At last, Lucy said, "I shall be glad to assist Miss Marlowe in her campaign to find a husband. Ordinarily, I would have nothing to do with a mercenary plan of this sort, but in her case, because she is so deserving and her future is so uncertain, I believe it is the only way. I mean to do what I can to enable her to find a life's companion who will care for her and love her."

Putting his hands behind his back, Edward frowned at the carpet. Then, looking at Lucy, he said, "Miss Bledsoe, your judgement is as sensible and feeling in this instance as it is in all others. I shall do what I can to help Susanna, and if I expressed myself too warmly against the idea earlier, I apologize. I hope I did not offend you."

Lucy shook her head. "You did not offend me. I only wondered what you intended to do with Miss Marlowe if you did not intend to let her marry. But I see you have changed your mind."

Lady Philpott clapped her hands. "Splendid!" she cried. "If the three of us are on the lookout for a husband, she is sure to succeed. I say three months and everything will be settled."

"But he must be a kind and gentle man," said Lucy.

"And rich," added Lady Philpott. "I won't absolutely insist on a title, though I have always like being a ladyship very well, but there must be money."

"He must be a man Susanna can respect," Edward said. "If he is dull, humourless or silly, she will be miserable."

"He must be a man of character," said Lucy in a quiet voice.

Excited, Lady Philpott said, "And handsome. Why should he not also be handsome, if he can possibly be?"

"He must be educated," Edward added. "Susanna is too accomplished in languages and literature to take pleasure in the company of a man who is ignorant and stupid."

Stunned, Susanna looked from one to the other. It had never occurred to her when she'd broached the subject of her marriage that it would come to this. Her only thought had been to make peace. She'd only wanted to ease her friends' worries. And now they were joining forces to palm her off on some ogre of a husband. Clearly, she ought to have kept silent, but it was too late. Oh, would she never learn to hold her tongue!

"There is to be a subscription concert on Tuesday," said Edward. "I shall go and see who has lately arrived in Bath."

"We shall *all* go," said his aunt. "I like a baritone as well as anybody, and three pairs of eyes will do better than one in finding out who is eligible. Are you agreed, Miss Bledsoe?"

"I will help if I can," said Lucy.

"There! It is done!" announced her ladyship in triumph. Turning a fond look on Susanna, she went to her and clasped her to her powdery bosom.

Over Lady Philpott's shoulder, Susanna watched as Edward crossed the room and sat by Lucy's side. Within the space of a few seconds, he had won a smile from her.

"All will be well," her ladyship murmured into Susanna's ear. "Your friends will look after you."

CHAPTER SIX

THE STRANGER

AT LADY PHILPOTT'S DIRECTION, Susanna stood under the arch while her ladyship chatted with an old acquaintance. As she waited, Susanna observed the crowd of sedan chairs passing through the street and heard the din of the crowd streaming into the assembly rooms. The traffic grew more and more tangled as chair men drew up to the arches along the building, deposited their modishly dressed inmates and inched away.

In the midst of this congestion, a sedan chair stopped in front of Susanna. She watched as the linkboy opened the door for the passenger. Out stepped a gentleman dressed elegantly in black pantaloons, a black coat and a crisp white cravat. At first, he appeared to be quite old, for his hair was silver, but when he emerged from the chair and glanced up, the light of the boy's torch caught his well-formed countenance, and Susanna saw that he was years younger than her father and very fine looking.

The gentleman reached into his pocket, apparently to pay the chair men, and when he did not find his purse, exhibited considerable irritation. After some time spent in searching, he seized the linkboy by the collar, nearly causing him to drop his torch, and he said in a voice loud enough for Susanna to hear, "You little demon! You have picked my pocket!"

The linkboy, who did indeed resemble a demon, rolled his eyes in an attitude of innocence and swore he had never so much as touched a finger to his worship's person. He invited the gentleman to search him up and down if he didn't believe him.

The gentleman smiled cynically, saying, "You've tossed it to one of your brother thieves, I daresay." Pushing the boy from him, he informed the chair men that if they wanted their money, they would jolly well have to get it from the linkboy. A babble of protest from the four men rose above the noise of the crowd. They pressed close to the gentleman in a threatening manner, giving the linkboy an opportunity to slink off and lose himself in the crush. Although the gentleman wore an attitude of perfect insouciance, Susanna began to fear for his safety. The chair men shook their fists in his face and vowed to relieve him of his watch, his ring and his ability to reproduce the species.

Susanna stepped forward and pushed two of the men apart so that they were forced to let her through. Opening her beaded miser's purse, she took out the entire contents—a bit of pin money Lady Philpott had given her—and put them in the gentleman's white-gloved hand.

"There. You may pay these men," she said.

He appraised her, admiring her gown of white gauze and silk mantle. "A beautiful damsel to the rescue," he said. He paid each of the men, saying, "Fortune smiles on us, lads."

Praying that no one had seen her give a stranger money, Susanna turned away to look for her ladyship. A minute later, the gentleman came after her. He stopped her by putting a hand on her arm. When she turned to look at him, he said, "You mustn't disappear before I am allowed to thank you."

She looked at the hand on her arm. Slowly, he removed it.

"Will you marry me?" he inquired.

After one astonished glance into his laughing face, she rushed off in search of Lady Philpott.

EDWARD AND THE BLEDSOES greeted them in the concert room and led them to a bench. Susanna found herself seated between Mr. Bledsoe and Edward. As she had already addressed to Mr. Bledsoe the two questions that at present formed the whole of her store of polite conversation, she turned to Edward. Before she could speak a word to him, however, she saw Lady Philpott beckon him to her, saying in a whisper, "Leave the seat vacant, Nephew. I shall see if I may persuade Lord Blessington to have it. After all, that is what we are come here for, is it not?"

Edward did not find another bench. Instead he took up a place by the wall. From that vantage point, he gave Susanna a heartening smile. In a few minutes, Lady Philpott arrived with his lordship. She bustled him into the vacated seat and sat on his other side. Lord Blessington greeted Susanna cordially with, "How do ye do, Miss Marlowe?" and then spent the next several minutes scanning the room for Miss Hargreaves.

Not for long did Susanna have to endure his lordship's inattention. The singers soon took their places by the musicians and began to fill the room with the melody of a lively Italian song. Susanna was captivated by the soprano, who tossed her head and gestured gracefully, giving expression and character to her interpretation. Too soon, it seemed, the end of the first act was announced and all were invited to take refreshment in the outer room. Susanna walked out with Lord Blessington.

She found that Lucy, Edward and Lady Philpott kept their distance from her. Their object, she knew, was to permit her to work her charms on Lord Blessington. She studied his lordship's eyes as they darted about the room in search of some young lady or other besides herself, and she despaired.

Hearing her sigh, Blessington inspected her. "Are you well, Miss Marlowe?" he asked.

She nodded. There followed a pause, during which her companion speculated as to whether Miss Murchen-Hill might be found in the crowd. He was certain he had spied her earlier.

Tearing her eyes from his face, she saw her friends watching her. She knew they would not like it if she let Lord Blessington get away. Therefore, she bestirred herself to speak.

"Tell me, my Lord," she said, "are you pleased with Bath?"

He seemed surprised by the question, as though no one had ever put it to him before. After some thought, he said that he had to confess he was not entirely pleased with the place. He had a single but strong grievance, namely, that his acquaintance were nearly always engaged and never at home when he called.

When she was sure that he had done answering, Susanna took a breath and asked, "Have you a large acquaintance in Bath?"

This question inspired his lordship to give more thought to Bath than he had heretofore. As he answered, he soon began to smile in self-satisfaction. At the end of three minutes, he was quite in charity with the watering place, for as he counted his acquaintance one by one, he realized that the total was enormous. The sheer number of them enabled him to overlook the fact that they were nearly always engaged and never at home when he called.

"This is remarkable," his lordship said. "I don't know when I have ever had so much conversation at one time."

Meeting his eyes, Susanna found him staring at her with a light that smacked strongly of admiration. Her friends would be pleased that she had done so well, she thought. But she could not be pleased. The only thing that would please her at this moment was her companion's absence.

"I believe I see Miss Hargreaves," she said.

He did not move his eyes from her face. "Miss Hargreaves is well enough," he said, "but she has no conversation."

Susanna tried once more. "I am certain I saw Miss Murchen-Hill on the far side of the room. Did you wish to pay her your respects?"

Lord Blessington gazed at her and shook his head. "I shall not leave your side for the likes of Miss Murchen-Hill," he declared staunchly.

If she did not get a moment away from him, Susanna thought, she would probably end by staring rudely at his nose, which, she noticed, drooped towards his curved chin. To prevent this calamity, she begged a cup of tea. With a bow and a parting look of ardour, he set forth on his quest.

Susanna inhaled a breath of relief and heard a soft laugh behind her. She turned to see the gentleman in black.

"I thought you would never get rid of him," he said. "I daresay you thought so, too."

"I hope I did not get rid of him only to be accosted by a stranger. You will make me regret that I ever assisted you."

He followed her when she stepped away. "You don't compare me to him, I hope. That fellow is an ass, whereas I am perfectly serious. Will you marry me?"

Susanna coloured and looked down. Just then, Edward approached. He studied the gentleman in black for some time. Then, taking Susanna to one side, he asked in a low voice, "Why did Blessington leave you by yourself? He ought not to have done so. He has exposed you to unwelcome attentions."

"Oh, Edward, I said everything to him that I could think to say. My only recourse was to ask him to fetch some tea."

Edward turned and pointedly gave the gentleman in black a warning glance, one that was returned with a smile and a smart bow before he walked away.

"Who is that?" Edward asked, watching the man's elegant retreating figure.

"I don't know."

"But he spoke to you."

"It was of no consequence, Edward."

But Edward was not to be comforted by such reassurance. He was too angry. "He would not have dared to speak to you if Blessington had stayed where he ought."

"If Blessington had stayed, something dreadful might have happened," she said.

He regarded her intently. "What do you mean? Did he insult you? Did he take any liberties? Tell me, Susanna."

"He behaved like a gentleman, I assure you. Only I kept wondering about his nose. It nearly dips into his chin, which is amazingly long. If one could pull his nose down and his chin up, they would meet."

Edward laughed. "You did not endeavour to introduce them to each other, I trust."

"You know very well I didn't; you have been watching me the whole evening. Edward, I am doing my best to behave myself as a lady should, but it is very difficult sometimes."

This speech gave him enough reassurance to make him smile. "You are well, I see. I ought not to have worried."

"Oh, but you ought to worry. I had to send his lordship in search of tea to keep from disgracing myself. What shall I do next time?"

Patting her hand, he said, "You are managing beautifully. If you do not wish to have Blessington for a husband—and I hope you do not—you may still converse with him. The practise may stand you in good stead at a later date."

Here the end of the intermission was announced, and the crowd began to flow to the concert room.

"Will you sit with us?" Susanna asked Edward. "I do not like to see you standing by yourself at the wall."

"My aunt has reserved the seat next to you for an eligible suitor. Besides, I can see you very well from where I stand."

Laurence Bledsoe, on his way back to the concert room, paused to greet them. With a bow, Edward excused himself.

For a moment, Susanna watched him go. At last, she was recalled to attention by the young Mr. Bledsoe, who assured her that drinking at the Hetling Pump had proved a miraculous restorative, though the fumes had nearly caused him to faint.

"I am glad you are feeling better," she said.

His response to this open expression was to step nearer to her. "Now you must tell me about yourself, Miss Marlowe. How do you get on in Bath?"

"I shall need a restorative more powerful than the Hetling Pump provides. I do not know how long I can sustain it."

"Sustain what?"

"The pretence that I am a lady," she said.

"Of course you are a lady."

"Hasn't your sister told you?" Susanna asked.

"I am at a loss to understand your meaning."

"I am very sorry. I thought they must have made you privy to their plan. They are all in on it."

He looked deeply concerned as well as puzzled. "What plan?"

"I am to be married. I am to act the part of a lady until I can catch a husband. If I fail to catch one in three months' time, I shall be a wretched pauper with nothing to live on, and heaven knows what will become of me."

Laurence Bledsoe blinked. "I hardly know what to say to such a dire prediction," he answered.

"I ought not to have told you. You have enough to bedevil you at the Hetling Pump without my burdening you with my troubles, and I must learn to hold my tongue. It seems I never do it when I ought."

He studied her solemnly for a time and made no reply. From his silence, Susanna deduced that she had shocked him. She warned herself not to be surprised or disappointed if his visits to her were curtailed henceforth.

Lucy came up then, and her brother took advantage of the opportunity to return to the concert room. When he'd gone, Lucy complimented Susanna on her beauty. Susanna would have returned the compliment had not Lucy interrupted to ask, "Who was that gentleman who spoke to you?"

Susanna blushed. She now heartily regretted having given way to the impulse to rescue the gentleman. Her intention had been to save him from imminent attack by ruffians. Her reward, however, had been mortification. "He is a stranger," she answered.

"He has a remarkably fine air and countenance," Lucy observed.

Susanna did not reply.

"Who was it who introduced you?" Lucy asked.

"You will be disappointed in me, I know, for I must confess, the gentleman and I have not been introduced. He took it upon himself to speak to me. I am aware it was improper of me to answer, but please do not blame me."

Lucy became distressed. She took Susanna's hand to say, "Do not think I meant to scold you, my dear. I was only curious about the gentleman. I wondered if perhaps you knew his name."

Susanna shook her head. She did not know his name and wished she might never hear him mentioned again.

But her wish was not to be granted, for Lady Philpott arrived then, and with her was the very gentleman they had been speaking of. The young ladies were presented to Sir Vale Saunders, whom Lady Philpott had known these hundred years at least. Susanna nodded and avoided his bold glance. Lucy curtsied and immediately engaged him in conversation.

"Are you fond of music?" she asked him.

He appraised her boldly and answered, "I am fond of being in the company of those who are fond of music."

"In that case," Lucy replied with a gaiety Susanna had not heard before, "I must tell you, I am very fond of music."

Lady Philpott, who had disappeared into the concert room as soon as she had captured and presented Sir Vale, now returned with Mr. Bledsoe and Edward in tow. Both were then given the honour of meeting Sir Vale. Edward greeted the gentleman stiffly, and stood quietly by, looking grave. But Lucy's father, who had ascertained from her ladyship that Sir Vale was a fifth baronet worth twelve thousand a year, could not say or do enough to make himself agreeable.

At this juncture, Lord Blessington arrived with Susanna's tea. The first-act interval was drawing to a close. The crowd was filtering back into the concert room. Susanna was exhorted to take her seat as quickly as possible. Lady Philpott assured Lord Blessington that Miss Marlowe could not possibly drink tea now and sent him off to return the cup. Thanks to this manoeuvre, it fell out that Sir Vale was given Blessington's seat on the bench next to Susanna. Not to be thwarted, Blessington returned to the concert room and dislodged several music lovers in order to squeeze into the seat on the other side of the young lady whose conversation he had discovered to be a marvel.

As the singing resumed, Susanna tried not to be aware of the expressions aimed at her. Ardour darted at her from the right, amusement from the left. Resolutely, she paid no heed to them. The one expression she could not ignore, however, was Edward's. He stood by the wall in the shadow of a dim light, his dark hair and watchful eyes shaded from view. Nevertheless, she could tell that he was unhappy.

She began to wonder if she had done something to distress him. It was very possible, even likely, that she had, for she had allowed the stranger to speak to her, and she had responded to his words when she ought to have walked away. Edward had seen the entire episode. Naturally, he disapproved.

The consciousness of his eyes on her warmed Susanna's cheeks. So long was she conscious of the sensation that after a time she felt she must be imagining it. To ascertain the truth, she turned to meet his look. He inclined his head to her in a curt bow that confirmed the fact that he had been steadily gazing at her. She looked down at her hands and wished she knew what his look signified.

LADY PHILPOTT WOULD NOT PERMIT Susanna to take her usual walk along the canal. They would soon be receiving callers, she cautioned, and not for the world would she disappoint the visitors by allowing Susanna to go out. Her ladyship did not have to wait long before a knock was heard at the front door and a caller announced, but the visitor proved to be only Laurence Bledsoe. He was relegated to Susanna's care so that Lady Philpott might stand at the window, on the alert for a more desirable caller, and while the two young people sat at backgammon, she peered between the curtains and sighed at the paucity of passersby along Sydney Place.

Laurence Bledsoe picked up the dice, shook them in the cup but did not throw them. Instead, he leaned towards Susanna and said in a low voice, "I have been thinking every minute of what you told me last night."

She, too, leaned forward and spoke quietly. "I am glad it did not dissuade you from paying me a visit. I was afraid you would think me too disgraceful to know."

"I hope I am not so disloyal a friend as that."

At first she did not know how to reply. His declaring himself her friend gratified her too deeply for speech. At last she smiled, remarking, "That was so very prettily said, Mr. Bledsoe, that I am almost persuaded to let you win this game."

"I mean to win without your letting me," he said. "I am beating you soundly already."

"I accept your challenge, sir," she replied.

Here his cheerful aspect faded, and he regarded her with the profoundest regret. "I don't have to tell you, I suppose, that I am a sorry, sickly fellow," he said.

"You are nothing of the sort," she contradicted. "Anyone who was sorry and sickly would not beat me at backgammon as unmercifully as you are doing."

"I am serious. My chronic complaints are such that I have a lifetime of them to look forward to. It is a circumstance that some time ago led me to resolve never to marry."

She swallowed, suddenly conscious that this confession was meant for her. With a smile and an air of lightness, she replied, "I see. It is your intention to warn me that I had better not set my cap for you."

He was horrified at the suggestion. "I never meant to suggest that you were setting your cap for me. I hope I am not so ridiculous or conceited as to imagine such a thing. What I wanted to tell you was that I should like nothing better than to marry you and provide for you the rest of your life, but I do not dare. I cannot shackle anyone with such a burden as myself, and especially not you! But if there is ever anything I can do for you, you have only to ask."

She took a moment to compose herself, then shook her head. "Now I shall have to let you best me, for that was the noblest declaration I have ever heard. And if you go on in that vein, I shall soon dissolve in a fountain of sentimental tears, and then you will be in a pretty pickle."

"I am glad you are not angry. I was afraid you might throw a lily pot at me, as you once did to Wilfred Sharpe." He smiled.

Laughing, Susanna replied, "It is just as well that you cannot marry me. I should fall into scrapes and make your life a perfect misery."

"You will marry someone strong and healthy and worthy."

"And rich. Do not forget rich."

They exchanged another smile and would have continued playing had not Sir Vale been announced. His arrival put an end to the game, and soon Laurence Bledsoe took his leave.

Lady Philpott fidgeted for some time, seeking a reason why she might leave Susanna alone with Sir Vale. The gentleman at last came to her rescue by inviting the ladies to walk with him in the Sydney Gardens. Pleading her impatience with the beauties of nature, her ladyship declined. But she urged Sir Vale to show Miss Marlowe the cascades. Miss Marlowe was excessively fond of cascades, though she could not abide a cascade herself. Susanna was urged to put on her pelisse and hat, and when her ladyship had looked her over and tugged her ribbons this way and that, she pushed her out the door with Sir Vale.

The baronet wore fawn pantaloons, a deep green waistcoat and a black spencer. His black beaver was stark against his silver hair, and his expression was one of amusement.

In silence, they walked through the gate to the gardens and along a path until they attained a bed of large yellow roses. Here they paused while Sir Vale drew some coins from his pockets and took it upon himself to place them in Susanna's reticule.

"It is small repayment for saving my life," he said, "but until you agree to be my wife, it will have to do."

"This is very bad of you, Sir Vale. I will not be teased on the subject of marriage. Of all subjects, it is the one I am least able to laugh at."

"I am not laughing."

"Of course you are. Otherwise you would not ask a perfect stranger to marry you."

"I am endeavouring to make you less of a stranger," he said. "We should certainly become better acquainted if we were married."

"But you do not know me."

"I know you well enough to admire your courage and generosity."

Susanna sniffed one of the yellow roses and replied, "Courage and generosity may be very useful if one is Caesar and must govern the Gauls and the Britons, but it is no foundation for marriage. In marriage, there must be a common way of thinking, a valuing of similar things and a genuine affection."

"That is precisely what I am looking for," he said.

She stole a glance at him. "Looking for?"

"Yes. I am in Bath expressly to find a wife."

"Oh, how very odd."

"Why is it odd? I am nearly forty years old. I have amused myself with diversions until I am weary of them, and I now long for a quieter and more sensible sort of life."

"It is odd because I am in Bath to find a husband."

They regarded one another for a moment and then could not help laughing.

"You ought to marry me on the spot," he said. "That way we should both have done with hunting and being hunted on the marriage mart. We might get on with the business of amusing ourselves in earnest." Gallantly, he put out his arm, inviting her with his eyes to take it.

She inclined her head but did not take his arm. "I'm afraid I shall have to look you over a bit further before I accept your offer," she said. "For all I know, you may not be wealthy enough to suit my ideas. You may have debts, or more illegitimate heirs and mistresses than taste and tradition permit. I must know your character before I accept your arm, let alone your hand. I am given to understand that a man's character is what renders him a good husband or a bad, and I have been warned to be careful."

He made a noise of disgust. "Who warned you, I should like to know? Who has made you so wary, cautious and untrusting?"

"Miss Lucy Bledsoe," Susanna answered, "and if she has succeeded in making me wary, cautious and untrusting where you are concerned, I think she has done me no end of good."

"Miss Lucy Bledsoe. If I am not mistaken, she is the inordinately elegant young lady with the pale brother and the avaricious father."

"Inordinately elegant, you say? She is no more elegant than you are yourself."

"Perhaps that is why she puts me off. One does not like to see one's own distinctions rivalled in others."

They walked to a pretty fountain where marble cherubs splashed in the water and sunlight. "You are very strange," Susanna said to Sir Vale. "Elegance is to be valued and admired, wherever it is found."

"I am not strange, only vain. I do not like to stand next to a young lady who is more elegant than I. I like to be seen to advantage, you see."

"Ah, so that is why you have asked me to marry you. In me you see the perfect foil for your refinement and magnificence. Seeing us together, your acquaintance could not forbear remarking that you had condescended beneath yourself to take a perfect bumpkin for a wife."

Drawing her swiftly under the shade of a hawthorn, he said, "If I kissed you, you would know my meaning well enough."

She stepped away. "You will not kiss me, sir. I have not known you long, but I have learned that you are rough with your inferiors and careless of your safety. Not only are you vain, but you disdain in others the qualities that endear you to yourself. That is not a character which deserves kissing."

"Your reasons are all very rational," he said, coming closer, "but you have not said that you do not wish me to kiss you."

"If you must know, I do not wish it. I am learning to be a lady, and while I still have many lessons to commit to memory, I do know that it is a lady's part to make a gentleman wish to kiss her, but not under any circumstances to let him."

He laughed. "You do not need to learn a thing, my dear rescuer. You are quite perfect as you are."

Since meeting Sir Vale, Susanna had found that his words often bordered on impropriety and rendered her uneasy. But when he told her that she was perfect just as she was, it was the first time he had ever caused her to blush.

THEY RETURNED to Sydney Place to find Lucy and Edward impatiently awaiting their arrival. Edward, who stood near the window, spun round to look at them when they came in. He said nothing beyond the barest greeting and seemed preoccupied. Lucy wished to know what sights they had seen on their stroll.

"Roses, madam," replied Sir Vale. "We viewed the roses."

Lucy walked a few steps toward the baronet. "I wish I might have seen them," she said. "I am partial to roses."

"You would not have liked these roses," Sir Vale said.

"And why not?"

"They are very large. There is something inelegant, I am sure you will agree, about roses that are very large."

"I do not agree," Lucy replied, "but as I have not had the privilege of viewing these roses myself, I cannot tell whether they were elegant or not."

The debate on the inelegance of large roses went back and forth until Susanna suggested, "Sir Vale, if you will take Miss Bledsoe to see the roses, the question may be answered at once. They are not far from Sydney Place."

Lucy was agreeable to the suggestion, and Sir Vale was not averse to escorting the beautiful young woman to the rosebed. As soon as they were out the door, Lady Philpott clapped her hands and embraced Susanna. "It is more than I ever hoped for," she cried. "Sir Vale Saunders! Why I have seen a thousand snares set for him and he has evaded them all. I never dreamed he would like you, but I believe he does. I am sure he likes you, and if you take pains to make yourself agreeable, my dear, he will make you an offer before September."

"I do not see that it is anything to be in ecstasies about," Edward said.

Lady Philpott regarded him in astonishment. "And why not, tell me? He is our man. I am sure of it."

Slowly, Edward walked to his aunt. He glanced once at Susanna, then turned to her ladyship. "It is true that I am not personally acquainted with Sir Vale, as you are, but I am acquainted with him by reputation. He is said to be a rake and a libertine. Word has it that he was at Brighton, but some scandal there sent him here. He is too fashionable a fellow to come to Bath in the ordinary way."

Lady Philpott waved her hand as though chasing away a pesky gnat. "Well, and what of it? A bit of the rake and libertine always make a gentleman more interesting, I think."

"But it makes him a highly unlikely prospect as a husband."

"Pah!" her ladyship scoffed. "Sir Vale is rich, handsome, educated, wellborn, amusing and in a fair way to liking Susanna very well, if she will exert herself to please him. That is what we agreed were the necessaries. If he likes to be left to his own devices now and then after they are married, Susanna will overlook it, I'm sure."

"You are wrong, Aunt. Susanna will not be happy with such a man. You are wrong on every count but one. Sir Vale does appear to be rather taken with Susanna, and I do not like it."

"You did not like Blessington, either. You do not like anyone I put forward, Nephew. I daresay you would object to Sir Galahad himself, if he could be brought to Bath and introduced to our Miss Marlowe in proper form."

"I do not like Sir Vale. That is all."

"Well, I do like him, Edward," his aunt cried shrilly, "and you are not to interfere."

"I'm afraid I *must* interfere."

Lady Philpott grew incensed. "Oh, you must, must you? I suppose you think you can swoof into my saloon and dispose of her as you please. Are you proposing to buy her shifts and petticoats and stuff and pinafores and pattens and gloves? Have you any notion what these items cost?"

Edward looked at Susanna. Warmly, he retorted, "We are not speaking of cost."

"We are speaking of nothing else. Unless you propose to pay her bills yourself, then you may not object. Unless you are prepared to undertake the task of finding her a husband as good as Sir Vale, you have no right to interfere!" Indignantly, her ladyship then flounced from the room.

Susanna sat down on a prim little chair and watched as Edward paced. His face was hard as stone, a rather forbidding face to those who did not know him. At last he stopped, and with his back to her, he leaned a hand on the mantel. "Lady Philpott is right," he said at last. "I have no right to interfere."

"You have every right," she said softly. "You are my oldest and dearest friend."

"Then I beg you, Susanna, be careful."

She did not reply. Her silence induced him to look at her. "What I said about Sir Vale was no more than the truth. He is a dangerous man, and when he learns of your father and the scandal, he may try to make you his mistress. That is why you must promise me you will be careful."

"I will try," she answered, "but truthfully, I do not know if I am able to be careful. I have never been careful in my life. I have always been the most careless chit in the world, as you well know. What does one do in order to be careful?"

He pulled a chair near to her and sat. "I shall advise you as best I can. When you find that a word or a tone of voice or a gesture confuses or distresses you, you must come to me and tell me. In the case of Sir Vale, it is especially important."

She turned away, troubled.

"What is it? What is the matter?"

"There is something, Edward."

"Tell me. You know you may trust me."

"You will be unhappy. More than anything, I hate making you unhappy."

"I am already unhappy, unhappy because I cannot do more to help you, because you of all people are reduced to marrying in order to survive in the world, because I have no alternative to offer you."

"What I have to tell you concerns Sir Vale."

He rose. "I knew it. He has already tried to make you his mistress, hasn't he?"

She shook her head. "Worse than that," she said. "He has asked me to marry him."

CHAPTER SEVEN

A SURPRISE

"HE HAS KNOWN YOU less than a day!" Edward said.

"I mentioned that fact to him," Susanna replied. "It did not appear to daunt him, however."

"What did you say to his proposal?"

"What could I say? I treated it as a joke. Now I think on it, he must have been only joking."

Edward searched her face. "Why should he joke?" he asked. "Why should he not love you?"

Seeing him look so earnest, Susanna sat forward. It had not occurred to her that love played any part where Sir Vale was concerned. In her heart of hearts she believed the baronet was flirting. But perhaps she believed it because she wished to. If he was serious, then she would have to give serious thought to accepting him, and there was nothing she wished to avoid more.

In another moment, Edward collected his thoughts and said, "Perhaps you are right. Perhaps it was only a joke. A man of his character may carelessly utter a proposal of marriage in a teasing, meaningless sort of way, and a young woman is wise not to make too much of it."

"That is what I thought, too," said Susanna. "But he has proposed four or five times now, and I do not know how I shall keep my temper if he goes on."

"Four or five times?"

"Yes. He is on the hunt for a wife. He told me so."

"He told you that?" He levelled a frown at the cande-labrum standing on the harpsichord. "And what did you answer? Susanna, you did not tell him you were on the hunt for a husband?"

The nod she made caused him to examine the candela-brum again with deep gravity. "This is worse than I thought," he said.

"What do you think I ought to do?" she asked.

He considered for some time, then asked, "Do you want to marry him, Susanna? If you loved him, really loved him, I should endeavour to remove my objections."

She stood and walked to the bright bay window over-looking the street. "I do not love him, but I do not expect to love the man who is to be my husband. If he is kind and keeps me from starving, I shall be content."

"But *I* shall not," he said, rising and following her. "You ought to love and be loved."

"You demand too much!" she cried, facing him. "You want me to catch someone in the space of a few months, someone who is perfect in every way according to your lights and Lucy's and Lady Philpott's, and you want me to love him into the bargain."

He steadied her trembling frame by placing his hands gently on her shoulders. In a quiet tone, he spoke her name, but he could not calm her.

Evading his look, she said in a quavering voice, "I don't know any longer what I am expected to do—whether to make Sir Vale love me or not, to persuade him to offer for me or not, to get him to marry me or not."

He pulled her to him so that her cheek rested against his, and for a moment, she had the luxury of feeling his com-forting touch on her hair. The next moment, however, the voices of Lucy and Sir Vale were heard at the entrance, and when they came in, they found Edward where they had left him, standing in a sunbeam near the window, and no Susanna to be seen anywhere.

WHEN HE HAD ESCORTED Lucy to Marlborough Buildings, Edward walked back to his lodgings. His route took him through busy Milsom Street, where he was shouldered and elbowed by the shoppers. He did not heed them, however. Nor did he heed the acquaintances who shouted and waved to him. At last, a sudden shower of rain woke him from his brown study, and he sought shelter in Mollands, which was warm with the aroma of pastry. He took a chair in the corner and wondered what the deuce he was going to do about Susanna.

Her passionate questions came back into his mind and worked on him forcibly. Of course she was confused. Of course she did not know what was expected of her. Of course she did not know whom to believe. He had confused her. Without meaning to, he had done everything in his power to confuse her. He had advanced arguments that contradicted his stated intention to assist her in the hunt for a husband. He had taken advantage of her loyalty and friendship. He had played on her partiality for him, knowing that his wishes would carry greater weight with her than the combined wishes of everyone else.

He'd done all that without knowing precisely what his wishes were. Yes, he wanted Susanna to be well provided for, and he did acknowledge that a husband would be the best means of accomplishing that end. But he resisted the idea. He found it distasteful in the extreme, not only because it enraged him to see a young woman of ability, charm and goodness without any other recourse, but also because the young woman in question was Susanna.

A picture took shape in his imagination. He saw Susanna brought into her new house, not a small, inferior house by any means, but a large, dark and gloomy one, like Edenhurst, which had frightened her as a girl. Behind Susanna, he saw a shadow loom—her husband, a man a good deal older and taller than his new bride, a man whose voice was silky, whose manner was seductive and whose eyes were sinister.

Edward acknowledged that the picture was overblown, fully worthy of one of Mrs. Radcliffe's novels. But it showed him more clearly than he'd seen before what his own fears were, and he resolved to cast about him until he found a way out for Susanna, some means of survival that did not depend on her marrying. Once he had done that, he might rest easy in his mind again. Once he had done that, he might attend to Lucy, whom, in recent days, he had neglected abominably.

DURING THE WEEKS that followed, Lucy Bledsoe got up several expeditions that, in addition to her family and friends from Cheedham, always included Sir Vale. Indeed, so many merry plans were made and carried out, that Lady Philpott complained of having scarcely enough time to scout the Pump Room every day for new arrivals. But as her principal reason for scouting the Pump Room had been answered by Sir Vale's attentions to Susanna, she was content to limit her complaints to only six or seven an hour.

One of the expeditions took the party to the Sydney Gardens on a warm, cheerful evening. The music, singing, cascades and illuminations put her ladyship in mind of Vauxhall, and she allowed the party to wander about the gardens with very few animadversions on the tediousness of natural beauty. And although she herself thought that half a mile of shrubbery was excessive, she professed a great admiration for the Labyrinth, in which, she pointed out significantly, lovers might lose their way for hours and hours.

Taking this hint, Sir Vale invited Susanna to explore the maze, and by dint of Lady Philpott's devices, which succeeded in delaying the rest of the party, the two were left to find their way through the Labyrinth themselves.

"This is the first opportunity I have had of late to speak with you alone," said the baronet.

Susanna replied that it was true; they had all been very much together.

"Lord Blessington is a great favourite with Lady Philpott, I collect," he said. "Is he an aspirant for your hand?"

Susanna could not help smiling. "Her ladyship deems him an aspirant, if no one better turns up."

"And you, Miss Marlowe, do you deem him an aspirant?"

Susanna was stopped for a moment. It occurred to her now that in all this time, she had not given Lord Blessington a serious thought. Her heart had always clung to the hope that something would turn up to prevent her having to marry such a man. But, she was forced to admit, she had no idea what that something might be.

"You are silent, Miss Marlowe. Did you hear my question?"

"I did hear it, and I have been thinking what to answer. And my answer is no; in my view his lordship is not an aspirant, and I shall never be persuaded otherwise."

The gentleman appeared satisfied with this answer and went on to ask, "As to Mr. Laurence Bledsoe, whose regard for you strikes me as quite touching, is *he* an aspirant?"

With a shake of her head, Susanna indicated that he was not. "Mr. Laurence Bledsoe is all that is modest and kind and considers himself too poor in health ever to marry."

"An excellent fellow. Long may his illness plague him. Now, what of Mr. Edward Farrineau?"

Startled, Susanna paused and stared at the path. "He is certainly not an aspirant," she said. "He is my friend."

Sir Vale laughed. "You imply that anyone who was your friend would not do anything so cruel as to become your husband."

"Mr. Farrineau wishes to marry Miss Bledsoe," she said.

"Then why is he always looking at you?"

Susanna coloured as she protested, "It is not true."

"It is not only true, it is irritating."

"He is watching out for me, I suppose."

"To what purpose?"

"He means to see that I do not fall into any scrapes."

Coming close to her he asked, "What sort of scrapes are you likely to fall into?"

"Mr. Farrineau wishes to see that I am happy. He does not like the idea of my marrying just anybody."

As they resumed walking, the baronet asked, "And am I 'just anybody'?"

The turn the conversation was taking unsettled Susanna. Without thinking, she replied, "In Edward's view, you are worse than just anybody. He has heard of your reputation and he fears for my happiness if I should become Lady Saunders."

Sir Vale laughed. "He is very gallant to defend you against me. What does he imagine I will do to you?"

"His fear is that you will try to make me your mistress."

He came to a stop then. For a moment, he took advantage of the light offered by a tall gas lamp to admire her deep blue dress and spencer. Then he said, "Is it possible that you would consent to be my mistress?"

"It seems to me there is too little security in being a mistress," she answered. "I might have the same insecurity by remaining a lady's companion, and I should have a good deal less dependence and inconvenience."

Laughing, he said, "I suspected you would not agree to it, and that is why I did not ask before. But I am not inconsolable. I have made up my mind to marry, and if I must sacrifice my freedom to have you, I shall."

"I do not love you, Sir Vale."

"I don't mind that. I rather like it, in fact. Endeavouring to win your love will amuse me for a year or two. It will be a great relief from the dullness of town."

Susanna shook her head. "I do not think I can consider you aspirant," she said.

"But you must. I have never been refused by a woman."

"Then my refusal will have the benefit of enlarging your experience."

That rejoinder entertained him immensely. "I am determined to have you," he said. "What do you say, Miss Marlowe? In all seriousness, will you not have me?"

"If you please, I would rather not think of marriage now, or, indeed, ever."

He bowed gracefully, and as they walked round another bend that took them to a row of delphiniums, he said, "I am told by Miss Bledsoe that your situation is quite desperate. She cautions me that the particulars of your circumstances are not generally known in Bath, and so I will assure you of my secrecy. But she fears for your future, and I fear for it as well. If you do not marry, Miss Marlowe, what will you do?"

Susanna glanced up at him. "I shall become a governess," she replied. "I am fond of children."

"Children? Heavens, they are nothing but mischief. You would be miserable. You must be miserable. Children, indeed!"

"But you see, sir, my whole career these nineteen years and more has been nothing but mischief, so I am well suited to the position. If I cannot find a husband by summer's end, then I shall advertise for a position as governess."

He could not hide the fact that he was nettled. That she should choose to be the slave of brats and their demanding parents rather than Lady Saunders vexed him considerably. "I think you are serious," he said. Abruptly, he invited her to turn round and return with him to the gate. As they strolled, he said little that did not pertain to the twists and turns of the path, so that Susanna had much leisure to ponder whether she was indeed serious.

The idea of becoming a governess was one that recurred, no matter how many times she dismissed it. What made it so inviting was the thought of teaching the children as she wished she had been taught—with encouragement to investigate and invent. But, at the same time, the disadvantages of such a situation gave her pause. Governesses were women of respectable family, and since her father's scandalous ruin and flight, she was unlikely to be thought respectable. Even supposing that she could prevail upon Lady Philpott to find her a situation, an obstacle still stood in her way—a monstrous obstacle, namely, that a governess must not only govern the children, but she must govern herself—her temper, her opinions, her conduct. She must be guarded at all times, careful not to consort with the servants because she was not precisely a servant, and watchful of her employers' dignity because she was not quite of their caste, either. When had Susanna Marlowe ever governed her temper, her opinions and her conduct? When had she ever been guarded, careful or watchful of anyone's dignity, especially her own? No, she would not last out a month as a governess. It was folly to think otherwise.

She was too well educated, she knew, to be acceptable as a seamstress or washerwoman. That left only the position of wife to consider. She had followed this labyrinthine reasoning many times in recent weeks and always she came to the same conclusion: that she must think of marrying, and with all the practical good sense she could muster.

If indeed there was to be no escape, if indeed she was to marry, what would it mean? The prospect, she found upon reflection, was not absolutely repugnant. Her mother had been happily married to her father. Although their sudden elevation in wealth and position had frightened the simple woman, she had always found solace in seeing to the linens, watching over the bakehouse, darning her daughter's petticoats, turning her husband's collars and taking a quiet evening in front of the fire to read. It was very possible, Susanna conjectured, that she might find much to like in such a life.

If her husband was not a kindred spirit, if she could not love him as she wished to love a husband, if his was not the smile she dreamt of when she closed her eyes at night, she thought she might still be able to withstand it, so long as her husband acknowledged her independence of mind and indulged her lapses. If she could have these things, she thought, she might be tolerably happy.

She stole a glance at Sir Vale, whose profile was strong in the shadows and lamplight. She thought that he would very likely give her a great deal of independence, if only because he would want his own. He would not insist on having tyranny over her thoughts and opinions. And she was certain that he would be indulgent, for he had, on only their second meeting, said something that she had not forgotten, something that she would never forget, something that no one else had ever said to her: that she was quite perfect just as she was.

Sir Vale did not think she needed lessons to improve her manners. He thought her attractive enough to propose to at every opportunity, despite her resolute refusals. He did not think she needed riches. Lucy had told him of her circumstances and he wished to marry her, anyway. Sir Vale did not think her a hoyden. He thought her eminently kissable. These were inducements that made him very much an eligible aspirant, especially in contrast to Lord Blessington.

These considerations were soon interrupted by Edward, who approached and said, "Ah, there you are. We thought we had lost you forever."

All the others then appeared. Lucy Bledsoe had been particularly anxious to locate Sir Vale. "I should not wish you to miss the fireworks," she told him a little breathlessly.

"I saw them last year," he said with a yawn, "and the year before that and the one before that. I suppose one may see them from anywhere in the gardens."

"But the view is so much better from the balustrade," Lucy said. "Miss Marlowe, do you not wish to see the fireworks?"

As soon as Susanna answered that she had never seen fireworks and the display would give her much pleasure, Sir Vale suddenly conceived a desire to view the spectacle also. He was not permitted to walk to the balustrade in company with Susanna, however. Edward contrived to detain him and engage him in conversation. So successful was he in monopolizing the baronet's attention that the others soon let them lag behind.

Having taken the measure of Sir Vale and found him, much to his annoyance, to be well formed in countenance and bearing, Edward came directly to the point. "Susanna has told me that you wish to marry her," he said.

"I beg your pardon, Mr. Farrineau, but I must ask what your interest is in the matter. I have never heard that Miss Marlowe is a relation of yours."

"She is a friend, a childhood friend. We have known each other nearly all our lives. I look out for her."

"Are you or your family her guardians, then?"

"Not by law. We do try to look out for her, however."

"I see. It is all done informally. You do not have any legitimate power over her."

Edward resented the tone of the question but replied as cordially as he could, "I believe I exert a certain influence that is the natural result of long-standing and affectionate acquaintance."

Sir Vale's fine profile showed a slight smile. "But she may do as she likes."

Edward could not deny it.

"I might mention," Sir Vale pointed out, "that you have no right whatever to interfere in Miss Marlowe's concerns, just as you have no right to interfere in mine. But I choose not to see your interference as interference. I choose to see it as something else."

The baronet stopped and looked Edward full in the face. His smile was arrogant. Behind him, a sudden illumination brightened the sky and the noise of fireworks sounded.

Edward met Sir Vale's gaze steadily and waited.

"I choose," Sir Vale said, "to see it in the very best light—as love."

"What the devil are you saying?"

"Do not misunderstand me, sir. I speak of the most disinterested love, of course. I speak of friendship, loyalty, devotion, all those tedious things the poets sing of. You love Miss Marlowe as you would love—shall we say— a sister, and thus I am disposed to regard you as her brother, an irritating, impertinent, interfering brother, but a brother nonetheless."

"Why are you disposed to be so good-natured, may I ask?"

As they resumed walking, Sir Vale answered, "Because I would not give you a reason to turn Miss Marlowe against me. I would like to have it appear that you and I are on terms of respect. I fear that if it comes to a choice between the two of us, she would choose to listen to you, even though it is in her interest not to do so. For these reasons, I should like us to proceed on terms of goodwill."

More fireworks lit the sky. The blast of colour could not be seen over the treetops, only the flash of light. The sporadic noise grew louder as they walked.

Although Edward disliked Sir Vale's tone, he saw in his words the opportunity he had been seeking. If he could persuade the baronet to agree to a delay, he might win the time he needed to do what he could for Susanna, to discover an alternative to marriage. Even if she ended by choosing to marry Sir Vale, at least it would be because she wished to and not because she had no other choice. "As Susanna's brother, then," Edward said, "I should like to propose a bargain."

Sir Vale declared that he was more than a little interested in hearing the terms.

"The terms are simply these: if you will hold off proposing marriage for a month, I will hold off interfering. During that month, you may see Susanna as often as is convenient to you both. You may endeavour to make yourself so thoroughly known to her that she can judge for herself what sort of husband you will be to her. In my turn, I shall make no objection to you, say nothing in regard to your reputation, and offer no opinions as to your eligibility. In addition, I shall not put forward any one else as a suitor."

Another burst of light broke in the sky. This time a few showers of green sparks were visible. The gentlemen emerged through the gate of the labyrinth and saw the silhouetted figures of the crowd gathered on the balustrade.

"I see no difficulty with my part of the bargain," said Sir Vale. "Yours wants a little fattening, though."

"What more do you require?"

"You must stop looking at Miss Marlowe all the time."

Edward paused. "What in blazes are you talking about?"

"I am talking about your constant staring. I noted it the first night we met, in the concert room. You stood at the wall and watched her and never once looked at the singers. It is the same whenever we are at Sydney Place. You stand by the window and watch her. It is the same everywhere."

"I suppose a man may look at his friend if he has more than a passing interest in her concerns."

"Yes, but I do not like it."

"Why do you object to my looking at her?" Edward inquired. "I have engaged not to interfere. I have engaged to give you a clear field with her. Is that not enough? What harm is there in my looking at her, unless you are the jealous sort, who cannot abide knowing that someone else thinks of her—no matter how disinterested his thoughts may be."

"I do not deny that I am capable of jealousy," said Sir Vale. "So are you, I vow."

Quickly and without a word, Edward walked towards the balustrade. In an instant he had climbed the steps and joined the party, which gazed upward in wonder at the glorious display of showering sparks.

Soon Sir Vale caught up to Edward. "You did not answer me, Mr. Farrineau," he said.

Edward faced him. Although Sir Vale was slightly shorter, he felt the power of the man's will. The baronet was as calm as a horse trader accustomed to getting his price. Edward waited for the next spray of sparks to light the sky. When it did, he was able to say, under cover of the crowd's cheer, "I will do everything I promised to do, but I will not engage to stop looking at her. I will never promise that."

Sir Vale shrugged. "Well, if those are the terms, I suppose I must be content with them." With that, he put out his hand.

Edward looked at it with distaste. Then, after shaking it perfunctorily, he walked down the steps and into the dark.

No sooner did Edward separate from the party than Lord Blessington joined it. "I called at Sydney Place but you were not home," he said plaintively. "Then, as luck would have it, I remembered Miss Bledsoe's plan to take you to see the fireworks."

Her eyes fixed on the sky, Susanna did not say much to his lordship beyond a polite greeting. Blessington squeezed in next to her, displacing Lucy. Noting that Miss Marlowe looked upward, waiting for the next round, he did likewise.

"Come, Blessington," Lady Philpott whispered in his ear, "you must let Sir Vale stand here. He has stood in back long enough and must be permitted to see the fireworks."

Lord Blessington complained that he, too, had missed the fireworks, "for I was running here and there looking for you. I saw Miss Murchen-Hill and might have stopped to speak with her, but I did not. I came straightaway to find you."

Lady Philpott did not appear moved by his lordship's exhaustive swooping about. Her object was to plant Sir Vale next to Susanna, and although the son of an earl might be thought to be as good a catch as a fifth baronet, still her ladyship had her heart set on ensnaring the latter, and she did not scruple to offend the former in order to accomplish her end.

Lucy stepped back to stand next to Sir Vale. To Lady Philpott, she said, "Oh, the view from here is quite as good as from over there. I don't think we need inconvenience his lordship."

Lady Philpott frowned. Her manoeuvrings were not meeting with the success she had anticipated. The party had rearranged itself without her guidance, and to her way of thinking, they had made a shabby business of it. Instead of Susanna, Lucy Bledsoe stood by Sir Vale's side, and the two of them talked in a low whisper that could not be overheard, no matter how hard she strained her ears. Her nephew—the puppy—had gone off without explaining one word of what had passed between himself and the baronet. She thought herself abominably used by all of them and declared loudly that she regarded fireworks as only slightly less tedious than scenery.

While her ladyship fretted, Susanna marvelled at the display. She had never seen fireworks before, and she welcomed the relief they offered from thoughts of matrimony. Gazing at the sky, she was not obliged to see his lordship's nose reaching to meet his chin.

The next burst of light shone blue, green and crimson. It was followed, even before the sparks melted, by a comet of white light. Susanna gasped as the light shot across the black sky, but her gasp was not inspired by the beauty and noise of the pyrotechnics. When the light had caught the crowd, Susanna was almost certain she had seen a familiar face.

Anxiously, she waited for another flash to illuminate the throng. She had to wait some time, however, because the next several displays appeared very high in the sky and were merely pretty. Another white comet finally gave her the opportunity to confirm what she had seen. Yes, she had seen him. She had seen Wilfred Sharpe, and what was more, he had seen her.

CHAPTER EIGHT

SUBDUING THE ENEMY

IN ANSWER TO Susanna's urgent notes, Edward and Lucy came early to Sydney Place. Their colloquy was undisturbed, as Lady Philpott had braved the weather and gone out. The three young people gathered near the bow window, and without preliminaries, Susanna disclosed who it was she had seen the night before.

"What do you suppose he means to do in Bath?" Lucy asked.

"Would you think I flattered myself if I said he'd probably come expressly to plague me?" Susanna asked. She was embroidering a flower in a hoop, and as she posed this question, she stabbed the needle through a petal.

Edward smiled a little. "From everything we know of Mr. Wilfred Sharpe, he will end by plaguing you, even if that is not his express purpose in coming here."

"That is what I think," Susanna agreed. "He would like to lay the blame for 'Lily-livered Willy' at my door." She made a series of uneven stitches that had to be ripped out.

Edward concurred. "If he still harbours a grievance on that head, he may think to revenge himself by bending every ear in Bath with the tale of your father's disgrace. He will not scruple to say that you are a swindler's daughter."

Susanna put her sewing to one side. "Let him say what he will. I am not afraid."

"Bravo!" Lucy cried. "So much for Mr. Wilfred Sharpe and his revenge!"

Edward was not moved to celebrate. "It is all very well," he said, "for Susanna to be brave. But what about this husband of hers, whom we all have agreed is to rescue her from calamity? What will he think if scandal should get about?"

The two young ladies exchanged a doleful look.

"He will think Bath a good deal too warm for him, I daresay," Susanna mused. She picked up her work and sighed.

"Lord Blessington would not like a scandal," Lucy said.

"You are right," Susanna replied. "He would instantly give me up and go swooping off, as Lady Philpott would say, to find Miss Hargreaves and Miss Murchen-Hill. And if that were the result of Wilfred Sharpe's coming to Bath, I should have to teach myself to be grateful for it."

"Sir Vale would not prove so fickle," Lucy said confidently.

Edward glanced at her. "I expect Sir Vale is looking for a wife who does not come to him under a cloud of scandal and who will suit his lofty notions of his position in the world."

"He is not a proud man," Lucy said. "Indeed, he does not regard position in the least."

"And how do you know this?" Edward demanded. "I suppose he told you so himself."

"In point of fact, he did," Lucy replied.

He glanced out at the street, where raindrops made splashes and rings in the puddles. "May I inquire how he happened to make such a confession to you?"

Susanna looked up from her needlework to listen.

"Do you remember the walk we took some weeks ago to see the overly large roses?" Lucy replied. "It was then that I asked him whether Susanna's position in life might affect his regard for her. He vowed it would not."

Susanna saw Edward's lips harden as he said, "You discussed his feelings for Susanna? Lucy, you had no right."

Offended, Lucy cried, "How can you say so? Did you not discuss the very same subject with him, too, only last night? Was that not why the two of you stayed behind and nearly missed the fireworks?"

He would have retorted but Susanna interrupted to say, "We are forgetting our present object—Wilfred Sharpe. The fact is that he might have it in his power to set about enough scandal to frighten off even Sir Vale—scandal which, I am obliged to add, has much foundation in truth."

"Let me go and find him out," Edward said. "I shall discover what has brought him here and try to learn what sort of stay he means to make. Once we know the facts, we may proceed with a plan."

"Oh, dear, another plan," Susanna said.

Edward rose and went to her with a smile. "Don't despair. We will take our cue from Caesar: we will scout our enemy's strength, calculate our strategy and subdue him at the last."

On that, he took his leave, and from the bow window, the two young women observed him walk toward Pulteney Street, his greatcoat and tall hat soon becoming swallowed up in the drizzle.

Susanna sighed. "I never liked Julius Caesar."

"Do you fancy Sir Vale for a husband?" Lucy asked.

"It is too early to tell," Susanna said. "I hardly know him, and much of what I know baffles me."

"But he is a fine figure and very handsome, is he not?"

Susanna leaned forward in her chair to say, "But did you not tell me, when we spoke of Edward, that it is character which determines a man's eligibility as a husband and not his face or his figure?"

Lucy blushed. "Did I say that? I suppose I did."

"And you were right."

"Was I?" Lucy asked. "I no longer believe anything with such certainty as I did then, except that when a gentleman of Sir Vale's refinement, breeding, education and bearing conceives an affection for a lady, it must be well-nigh impossible to refuse him."

"It was not the tiniest bit impossible. I had no difficulty that I recall."

Lucy's eyes opened wide. "You refused him?"

"Several times."

"But how? Why?"

"I must remind you that you refused Edward. I have only gone and done the very same thing you did."

Slowly, Lucy stood and walked to the harpsichord. In its shiny, polished surface, she saw her reflection. "Lord, Susanna!" she exclaimed. "You were right. It is *exactly* the same thing!"

"Sir Vale is amusing and interesting, and I respect his understanding as well as his riches. I must add to these attractions his professions of admiration. Indeed, no one can resist being told that one is perfect just as she is."

"He said that to you?"

"Yes, but he goes too quickly and too far."

"He goes quickly and far because he is a man of the world. He knows his own mind, and his own heart."

"If he could be made to be patient, I should not feel so uneasy in his company. I cannot accept a man on so short an acquaintance. I am accustomed to knowing everyone forever and ever and to having them know me."

"You do not like him, then?"

"I can hardly tell. At times, when I am with him, I feel that I would only have to be myself to please him. I admire his humour, his grace and manners. I am awed by him, I confess. And I am flattered by his regard."

"I should feel exactly the same way, I daresay."

"But I sometimes think his elegant dress and manners make him difficult to know. Perhaps I am unaccustomed to such attentions from a gentleman, but I do not wish to mistake them for true character. As you see, I have not forgotten what you have said on the subject of character."

"I myself have wondered much about Sir Vale's character and am persuaded that he is everything a gentleman ought to be. I fear that if you dismiss him, Lady Philpott will be disappointed. Or worse, that she will be angry."

Impulsively, Susanna threw aside her embroidery and approached Lucy. "You will not be disappointed, will you?" she asked urgently. "I couldn't bear to disappoint you again."

Lucy's eyes filled with tears, and as she embraced Susanna, she took her oath that she would not be disappointed one jot if her friend did not marry Sir Vale Saunders.

EDWARD SET FORTH purposefully, not realizing until he had crossed Pulteney Bridge that he had no idea how to find out the direction of Wilfred Sharpe. He had not caught the announcement of his arrival in the newspaper and hardly knew how the fellow was to be discovered. At last it occurred to him that if an ailment had brought Wilfred to the spa, then he might be found in the Pump

Room, taking his regulation cupfuls each day. With the Pump Room, therefore, Edward resolved to begin.

Fortunately, it was not crowded. All the chairs were taken, but no one found it necessary to stand. Edward joined the ladies and gentlemen standing by the fountain, which gurgled forth the salubrious waters. Upon inspection, none of the faces he saw proved to be Wilfred's. Next he strolled the hall, studying everyone he passed. Wilfred Sharpe was not to be found.

When he left the building, it was still raining. He stood in the Abbey churchyard, thinking what to do next, when he spied Wilfred Sharpe at some distance. He saw the young man cross Cheap Street, and he followed. By dint of brisk walking, he soon caught up with his quarry. He greeted him and feigned surprise at seeing his old neighbour in Bath.

"I am now curate at Walcot Church," said Wilfred, not without some pride.

"I congratulate you," Edward said. "Then you mean to reside here, I collect."

"The position is only temporary, while the regular curate travels."

"How long do you mean to stay?"

"A month, perhaps longer."

"Well," Edward replied, "how very pleasant."

"Mr. Farrineau," Wilfred said, "it is an odd coincidence that we should meet, and also a handy one. I bring you a letter from Sir Dalton."

"You left my father well, I trust, and your own father, too?"

"Yes, they are very well. Sir Dalton arrives in Bath soon and sends you notice of it. But I must say no more. You must come to my rooms, and I will give you the letter."

The two gentlemen set forth towards Wilfred Sharpe's lodgings at the very bottom of the town, and when they were seated in the tiny room that served Wilfred and the other boarders as a parlour, Edward took the measure of his enemy. "You are perhaps aware that some of your old acquaintance from Cheedham have come to Bath for the season," he said.

"I am," Wilfred replied. "I have heard that Miss Susanna Marlowe resides in town." Here he frowned.

"You know very well that Miss Marlowe resides in town," Edward said. "You saw her last night at the Gardens, just as she saw you."

Wilfred shrugged. "Now I think on it, I believe I did see her last night."

Edward continued smoothly, "Her friends are glad she is not gone to Scotland and are pleased to look after her. You must know that we have the utmost concern for her welfare."

"Miss Marlowe is fortunate in having so many devoted friends. Yet it strikes me as very hard that she should have such friends while I, who have lived in Cheedham a great deal longer, should have none. Indeed, I have been in Bath for some time and have been thoroughly ignored by you all."

"We had no idea of your arrival."

"Had you known of it, what should you have done? Perhaps you would have thought a poor clergyman too humble to know. Or perhaps Miss Marlowe would have led you in sniggering at me and whispering that epithet which I abhor to mention."

"I doubt we should have given you much thought at all," came the amiable reply. "As to sniggering, I assure you, Miss Marlowe never called you by that or any other name in her life. She is not so spiteful as you are pleased to think; nor are any of us."

"I take that to mean that I may rely upon you to save me from perishing with boredom in this dreary place, that you and the others will be so good as to extend to me the same hospitality which you extend Miss Marlowe."

"What is it you are after, Mr. Sharpe? I wish you would tell me straight out."

With a shrug, Wilfred said, "I am after nothing, only a little attention from my old friends and neighbours. Heretofore, I have divided my time in Bath between this tiresome old room and a tiresome old church. I am heartily sick of both and require a little amusement. I do not see why my old acquaintance should not amuse me, and surely, you know of all the diversions the town affords. In addition, I should like to renew my acquaintance with Miss Marlowe, for there is nothing that would gratify me more than to know that the unfortunate creature has mended her ways and conducts herself properly in society."

"Tell me this, do you mean to set about gossip, Mr. Sharpe? For I warn you, if you intend to whisper about Miss Marlowe and her father's difficulties, you will have to deal with me."

"Ah, then you have contrived to keep it all secret, have you?"

"Do you mean to say anything or not, sir?"

Wilfred put up a hand to protest his innocence of any such intention. "You mistake me. I wish Miss Marlowe only the best of good fortune. But I believe my father's position, not to mention his long-standing acquaintance with your father, entitles me to the same courtesy you extend to the daughter of a swindler!"

"In, short," said Edward, "you are willing to trade your silence for the opportunity to associate with your betters."

Eyeing him insolently, young Sharpe replied, "I believe we understand each other very well."

Edward paused, then said, "I shall see what can be done."

AT THE VERY NEXT OPPORTUNITY, he presented Wilfred's demand to the ladies. It was still raining outside, had been raining for days and days now and the scheme of viewing the regimentals on the Royal Crescent had had to be abandoned. After explaining to Lady Philpott who Wilfred Sharpe was and what danger he might pose, Edward announced, "I believe he may be kept from doing harm, if we can bring ourselves to withstand his company."

"I don't see how such a person is to be kept from doing any measure of harm," said her ladyship, incensed at what she had heard of young Mr. Sharpe. "He sounds a very nasty little fellow who likes nothing better than to make himself disagreeable. I wish it were the old days, Edward, and you might call him out. The fellow deserves to have his throat cut. That is the only way to teach him a lesson, mark my words."

"I hope you are wrong," Susanna said, "for though I have never liked Mr. Wilfred Sharpe, I should like nothing better than to find a way of making peace with him."

"A truce is precisely what I had in mind," Edward said.

Lucy interposed here. "But both parties must honour a truce, and I do not trust Wilfred Sharpe to honour anything."

"It would be in his interest to do so," Edward said, "for he wishes to be noticed by us."

"Mr. Caesar would approve your cunning," Susanna told Edward. "He knew well how to make his enemies gallop to the treaty table."

He smiled. "I confess I am no Caesar, but I think the strategy may work effectively. What I propose is this: that we flatter Mr. Sharpe, invite him to visit, take him on an excursion, make him feel that we welcome his association. We may not only render him harmless as a result, but we shall be able to keep an eye on him, too."

"Lord Blessington proposes to take us all to Blaise Castle," Lucy said, "and it appears a pleasant enough scheme. Do you think that Wilfred Sharpe should make one of our party?"

"By all means," Edward said.

Lucy shook her head, endeavouring to imagine Wilfred Sharpe in the company of Lord Blessington and Sir Vale Saunders.

Susanna also shook her head, but for another reason. "I do not like the plan. I am very sorry, Edward, but you do not know what the outcome will be."

He approached her and lifted her chin so that her worried eyes met his. "Tell me why you object. Are you frightened?"

Susanna, who scorned to be frightened by such a fellow as Wilfred Sharpe, could not say a word, so conscious was she of Edward's hand on her face.

Removing the hand, he sat down next to her on the sofa. "You are not willing to forgive him. Is that it?"

Shaking her head, she said, "As soon as Mr. Wilfred Sharpe has the opportunity, he will do something or other to torment me. No doubt he will demand that I kiss him, as he has done before."

Edward's softness faded. Abruptly, he stood and walked to the fireplace. "Kiss you? He will try to kiss you?" He pounded his fist on the mantel. "I see that I have been far too sanguine," he said darkly. "I was wrong to believe the fellow could be brought to a bargain. Now I see that my aunt is right, and throat-cutting would be far more fitting than a truce."

"Oh, but your plan is excellent, Nephew!" exclaimed her ladyship. "If all the gentleman wants is a kiss from our dear Miss Marlowe, then he may be made tractable."

Her listeners stared, not comprehending either her meaning or her prodigious good cheer.

"It makes perfect sense," she said. "If he has conceived a tendre for the girl, she may tease him and flirt with him and drive him positively to distraction. He will be much too violently in love to think of harming either her person or her reputation."

Glances were exchanged and doubts expressed. Lucy was the first to allow that there might be some merit in her ladyship's reasoning, but she added, "I would not wish to pursue this plan of wooing Wilfred Sharpe unless Susanna were up to it."

"Of course she is up to it," Lady Philpott declared. "And whatever she doesn't know about driving a young man to distraction, I shall teach her."

Lucy regarded Susanna with some concern. "But it is so very unpleasant to have to make up to such a one as Wilfred Sharpe. I don't see how she will manage it."

"She will manage it," said her ladyship. "It will be excellent practise for becoming a wife, for there is nothing a wife needs to know so thoroughly as how to suppress her own likes and dislikes in order to rule her husband."

Susanna, who had not taken her eyes from Edward's serious face, said, "I do not mind so very much having to make up to him. But I am afraid I will not be able to control my temper. Suppose I should do something dreadful? Then everything will be lost."

"You fret too much," said her ladyship. "It is agreed. This is our plan: to disarm Mr. Wilfred Sharpe with our cordiality, and whatever questions you have, dear Miss Marlowe, you have only to ask me. I shall give you all my little secrets and you will be the most charming creature any pitiful man was every enslaved to."

In a quiet voice, Edward said, "No, Aunt. This cannot be. I won't have it." All the ladies glanced at him. "It is too dangerous. I do not foresee that Wilfred Sharpe will be put off by a mere show of hospitality, despite his promises. He has bedevilled Susanna all her life and he will continue to do so. Moreover, he will not stop at demanding kisses. I blame myself for ever thinking otherwise."

Lady Philpott went to him at the fireplace and shook her finger in his face. "You object to everything, Nephew! I declare, I am growing impatient with these objections of yours."

"Aunt, I cannot allow Susanna to be placed in such a position of danger. The situation must be so repugnant to her sensibilities that she will be made very unhappy. I cannot stand to see her made unhappy."

Lucy and Susanna looked from the nephew's earnest, intense face to the aunt's red and furious one.

"Edward," her ladyship hissed, "if you wish to be allowed into my house, if you wish to be permitted to voice your opinion regarding the disposal of Miss Marlowe, then you will not say another word. I will not be crossed!"

At this threat, Susanna stood up and came between the two relations. She had no hope of persuading either one to relent. Therefore, she said soothingly, "I should like nothing better than to drive Mr. Sharpe to distraction. Moreover, I should be grateful to learn a means of dealing with him that does not require throwing a lily pot at his head or dousing him with a pail of water.''

Edward stared off into the distance and Lady Philpott looked triumphant. Turning then to Edward, Susanna said softly, ''I should feel a good deal safer if we did keep an eye on Wilfred. Truthfully, nothing pains me so much as to hear people speak of my father's disgrace. Here in Bath, I have been spared that mortification. If the only way to continue in such a happy condition is to get on with Wilfred Sharpe, then I shall do it. But if he does end by broadcasting the West Indian affair or even if he just plagues me for kisses, I shall inform you on the spot and then you may cut his throat with my blessing.''

Edward was induced to smile.

''There. It is all settled,'' said her ladyship with satisfaction. ''And if I shouted at you, Nephew, I do apologize. It is only that on certain points you are obstinate and provoking. I imagine you take after your father.''

Edward laughed. ''I have strong opinions, I own. But I believe it is you I take after, Aunt, and not my father.''

Her ladyship blushed prettily and goodwill was restored.

WHEN EDWARD AND LUCY took their leave, and Lady Philpott and Susanna found themselves alone with only their sewing and their thoughts, Susanna put aside her work for a moment to ask, ''Lady Philpott, do you truly mean to teach me what you know of managing a gentleman?''

''Mean it! I should like nothing better. It would be a shame to take the secret with me to my grave.''

''I do not know how to manage, how to truly manage *anyone*, especially a difficult gentleman who insists upon kissing me.''

"Yes, that can be very trying. It has happened to me so many times, I cannot begin to count them."

"And you say you managed them. But how?"

Her ladyship pushed away the fire screen she was making and said confidentially, "What you must understand is that women do not merely manage the men. That is nothing. The idea you must grasp is that women manage the world."

Susanna inhaled and sat back. It had not occurred to her that women played such an important role in the universe. So far, she had seen only that women were constrained by their respectability to become either governesses, wives or spinsters, and if they had no income or family, spinsterhood was not an alternative. "How do women manage the world?" she asked.

"By managing the gentlemen."

"I see." But she did not see at all.

Lady Philpott warmed to her theme. "Women manage the men in this fashion—by conceiving an idea and planting it in the brain of a gentleman in such a manner that it takes root there and at last blossoms and flourishes."

"What sort of an idea?"

"Let us say that a wife wishes to have a new carriage and footmen in purple livery."

Susanna was all attention.

"Now it is to the husband's benefit to have such a carriage and such footmen, but he is too dull to know it. It is therefore his wife's duty to educate him."

"I have it," Susanna cried. "She expostulates with him in the most sensible manner, giving him all the reasons why such an expense will be to his benefit."

"Don't be ridiculous," her ladyship cried.

Chastened, Susanna said no more.

"She comes upon her lord during an auspicious moment, when he has eaten a good dinner that she has caused to be made for him and after she has brought him a good cigar and a glass of port. But she does not expostulate with him. No, no. That would be the height of folly, for the last thing a gentleman wants to hear from a lady is her reasons for a thing."

"What does he want to hear?"

"He wants to hear what pertains to himself. Therefore, the lady says to him, 'Have you seen Lord Such-a-One's new carriage?' He naturally answers that he hasn't because Lord Such-a-One has no new carriage, the lady having invented the whole thing. But her husband has always envied Lord Such-a-One, so he takes his nose out of his newspaper and asks, 'What new carriage?' She then describes the very equipage she wishes to have."

"And what does he answer?"

"Nothing, for she then goes on to ask if he has seen Lord Such-a-One's liveried footmen. Precisely the same conversation takes place on this subject, and then the husband says, 'Why should Lord Such-a-One have such a carriage and such exquisitely liveried footmen and not I?' His wife, taking his part as a good wife should, tells him he deserves such bounties every bit as much as Lord Such-a-One, nay, even more, for he is the noblest and worthiest Englishman born. 'I say, I have an idea,' the husband announces. The wife patiently waits while he explains to her what he means to buy in the way of a new carriage and how he means to dress his footmen henceforth. And that is how it is done."

Susanna said not a word.

"Do not be awed," said her ladyship kindly. "It is an art, I own, and an exacting one, but you will learn it in time."

"I am not awed," said Susanna. "I am appalled."

"Well, that is much like being awed, I think. You will soon catch the knack. You are a quick study."

"But why should it be a woman's task to induce a gentleman to do what he never wished to do?"

"Why, because it is best for him."

"Does a man not know what is best for himself?"

"If he did, do you suppose I should be Lady Philpott? My dear girl, his lordship never had a thought of marrying a poor girl with an indifferent education and the smallest possible claim to beauty. He married me nevertheless, and I can tell you, we were as happy as any two people can be and still be married."

"I do not know what to say," Susanna confessed. And, indeed, she was speechless, for the notion that it was a woman's part to seduce a man into her way of thinking made her fear for the safety of England, the order and stability of the world and the outcome of her first meeting with Wilfred Sharpe.

CHAPTER NINE

THE FOLLY

THE MEETING with Wilfred Sharpe was to take place shortly, just as soon as it should have stopped raining and the sun had dried the ground and made the roads fit for travelling. At that time, the excursion to Blaise Castle was to go forward, and Wilfred had agreed to form one of the party.

Too soon for Susanna's comfort did the rains begin to abate. One day the sun nearly threatened to find its way out of the clouds, and four days later, it succeeded in achieving that end. The chill air was warmed. The earth began to dry. The mud and puddles disappeared. And the day arrived when the long-anticipated expedition was actually to come to pass.

Before the carriages could set forth in the direction of Bristol, Susanna was required to greet Wilfred Sharpe in Lady Philpott's parlour. She performed the duty with as much cordiality as she could assume but found little to say to him. He kept his eyes low and humble. From time to time, however, he stole a glance at her that betrayed certain thoughts not generally associated with curacy. While the others of the party planned the day's outing, Susanna and Wilfred were left to entertain themselves, which they did in excruciating silence.

At last, Susanna recollected her lessons. She smiled pleasantly and asked, "Are you pleased with Bath?" which Wilfred answered with a shrug. This question was followed by its customary companion, to which the curate replied that his old friends from Cheedham had proved unaccountably neglectful thus far and he hoped they now meant to pay off every arrear of civility. Susanna knew not how to respond to such a statement and experienced considerable uneasiness until the time for departure arrived.

Hurrying from the house, Susanna allowed Lord Blessington to hand her into his open curricle. Lady Philpott was vexed to see Susanna disposed of in such an unsatisfactory manner. She observed Sir Vale, standing alone by his curricle, watching Lord Blessington fawn over the young woman he had thought to drive himself. Her ladyship waxed even more irritated when she saw Lucy Bledsoe approach Sir Vale, and after some minutes spent endeavouring to win his attention, succeed in being invited to take the passenger seat in his curricle.

Lady Philpott, whose carriage could accommodate six at a squeeze, was left to drive the remainder of the party. She sat next to Wilfred Sharpe and opposite them sat Edward. Thus they drove to Blaise Castle, with Lord Blessington's curricle well in advance of the others. As his lordship had seen Blaise before and was familiar with the route, he was allowed to be the guide for their excursion.

Lord Blessington and Susanna talked of his lordship's numerous acquaintance in Bath. He was able to tell her, without her even asking, the names of all the young ladies he had danced with in this and in all previous seasons; the names of their parents, siblings and relations; their ages; and the number of seasons they had seen in London. While his lordship entertained her in this manner, Susanna was at liberty to occupy her thoughts elsewhere, and they had no want of subject. From the moment she had set eyes on Wilfred Sharpe's face, she had been unable to shake a peculiar sense of dread. Her thoughts could not be said to be very clear. She knew only that she was filled with a vague foreboding and that it went beyond the fear that he would frighten off her suitors with talk of the West Indian scandal.

In the carriage, meanwhile, Lady Philpott and Wilfred kept up a flow of conversation. Her ladyship had found in the young curate a kindred spirit who regarded hills and dales, shrubs and trees, view and prospects, streams and canals, flowers and herbs, ducks and swans, birds and butterflies—in short, all of nature's pageant—as tiresome as she did. In consequence, she forgot to dislike Wilfred Sharpe as much as she had intended. If she could not sigh over nature's wonders, which they passed frequently en route, she could share with Wilfred the far greater pleasure of despising them whenever they hove into view.

Edward watched and heard everything, pleased that Susanna rode safely ahead in another carriage. He fully intended to stick close to the young curate and to make certain he did not inflict his presence on Susanna. The idea that Wilfred had demanded kisses from her displeased him more and more each time he thought about it, and he thought about it often. Sitting near Wilfred, Edward had all he could do to content himself with merely keeping an eye on the fellow.

"We will like Blaise, I am sure," her ladyship confided to Wilfred. "It is a castle, after all. There will be much to see; we shall not be forced to march through woods and look at frog ponds. To my mind, there is nothing so dull as a frog pond."

MUCH TO HER DISGUST, Lady Philpott's prediction of delight was not borne out. Indeed, even Susanna was disappointed in what she saw, for the castle turned out to be merely a folly, built by a Bristol banker who had wanted something charming to see from his window. He had caused the structure to be built high in the trees, so that until the party had actually climbed the steep hill and Lady Philpott had exclaimed against so much infernal hiking, they did not know that what they were about to see was only a sham castle. When at last the party stepped into the clearing and saw a very neat but tiny folly in front of them, the truth began to dawn.

They walked once round the grey stone building to inspect the towers, an excursion that took less than a minute.

"Where's the rest of it?" asked Lady Philpott.

"Oh, there isn't any rest of it," explained Lord Blessington. "This is all there is."

Her ladyship shot him a look. "You forced me to climb all this way through all those trees, on all those stones, for a folly?"

Everyone, with the exception of Lady Philpott and Susanna, had known what Blaise was. Her ladyship taxed them with deceiving her and would not hear their explanations and apologies. "What have you to say for yourself?" she demanded of Lord Blessington.

"A pretty little folly, isn't it?" he said, swelling with importance at being the only one who had been to Blaise before. "Come along," he beckoned.

He entered the vestibule of the castle with the others following close behind. They toured the pretty dining and service rooms on the ground floor, admired the niches, plastcrwork and traceried windows in the main room and climbed the stairway in the north turret so that they might view the Bristol Channel from the flat roof. The entire tour took fifteen minutes, and when they had gathered on the lawn outside once more, they wondered what in heaven they were to do with themselves then.

"Shall we go and see the Woodland Lodge?" Lord Blessington invited, a suggestion that caused Lady Philpott to say gratefully, "Oh, yes, a lodge, where I may sit and have something to drink and get out from under this monotonous sunshine."

His lordship's face fell. "I'm afraid the lodge is not meant to accommodate visitors," he said.

"Does no one live there?" asked her ladyship.

"Oh, yes, but only to keep the fireplace tended. You see the owner likes to see the lodge from his house in order to have a view of a peaceful thatched cottage with smoke rising from the chimney. A clever idea, is it not?"

Lady Philpott glared at him. "Is anything real in this place, or is everything a sham?"

Wrinkling his brow, his lordship paused to think. "There are some fine woods hereabouts, which I believe are the original woods. And the trees are real enough, I expect. You may see holm oaks and Scots pines, I am told, though you must not ask me to point them out to you, as I do not know one from another."

"Look!" said Susanna, calling their attention to the edge of the cliff where she stood. "It is a lovers' leap."

The party moved near her. Taking in the delightful serene woods surrounding the cliff, Edward said, "There is a footpath just below. Shall we all go and see what this lovers' leap may lead to?" He jumped gracefully down a large stepping-stone and waited to see who would join him.

"You must be daft, Nephew," said Lady Philpott. She turned to Wilfred Sharpe and Lord Blessington. "I shall not go swoofing about in any woods," she informed them.

Then, announcing that they were to have the honour of assisting her down the way she had come up, she went off with them in the opposite direction.

Of the remaining party, Sir Vale was the first to move. "By all means, let us see what underlies Lovers' Leap," he said, and swiftly descending the rock, he reached out his hand to Susanna. With only the briefest glance at Edward, she allowed the baronet to jump her down. The two of them led the way along the path. Edward then helped Lucy down and together they followed.

As soon as they had rounded a bend and Edward and Lucy could no longer see them, Sir Vale said, "Miss Bledsoe tells me that your situation is more unfortunate than I knew. Forgive me for speaking of what must surely give you pain, but I wish to tell you how sorry I am that your father's disappearance has heaped the most dire and undeserved consequences on his daughter."

Susanna fixed her eyes on a spray of cowslips along the path. "I am obliged to you for your compassion," she said, "but you need not make my situation more pitiful than it is. I shall do well enough."

He removed his tall hat and held it in his hands. Susanna knew that so elegant and worldly a gentleman as Sir Vale was not readily moved. She was honoured that he had been moved in her case to express his sympathy.

"It is unjust that you should suffer for your father's fraud," he said.

"Your kindness will, I trust, make allowances for me when I say that I do not wish to speak of my father. Others may regard him as a fraud, but to me he is my father and always will be."

Respectfully, he remained silent for a time, then said, "I do not wish you to think that I have given up hopes of marrying you on that account."

She looked at him.

"If I were a young man, dependent on those who held power over my fortune, I should be required to hesitate. But I am my own man entirely. There is no one I am forced to answer to besides myself, no one's comfort or dignity I am obliged to consult besides my own. If you could manage to withstand the tongue-wagging that would follow upon our marriage, I certainly could, and I have no doubt that it should soon die down."

"I have not accepted your proposal of marriage, Sir Vale."

"No, but you will." His smile was slight but confident.

"I cannot marry you, sir."

"Ah, my dear, I have resolved not to press you on the matter just now. Two weeks hence, I shall renew my offer, but until then, you must be patient."

Susanna paused under a majestic beech that shaded the path. "Perhaps it would be best if you did not renew your offer. Although you profess to be content to marry a woman who does not return your regard, you cannot mean it. And even if you do mean it, I think well enough of you to wish you something better than that. Believe me, sir, nothing is so hurtful as loving where you are not loved."

Sir Vale looked grim for a moment, then asked, "Are you in love with someone else?"

She coloured.

"Ah, I believe I have hit upon the truth."

Unable to deny it, Susanna could not answer.

"May I ask the name of the fortunate gentleman?"

Before she could reply, Edward and Lucy rounded the bend and could be seen at the top of the path. Sir Vale looked at Susanna's face. He read instantly the expression that softened it as soon as she saw Edward. His eyes narrowed. Then he laughed. "You cannot be in love with Mr. Farrineau!" he said. "It is too ridiculous."

Mortified, Susanna brought her hand to her throat.

Edward had seen her now and had begun to walk faster in her direction.

Sir Vale shook his head. "It will not do, you know. It will not do. Mr. Farrineau is to marry Miss Bledsoe, I am told."

"She has not accepted him."

"Ah, but she will. And even if Mr. Farrineau were in love with you instead of Miss Bledsoe, he is not independent, as I am. Apart from the thousand pounds a year and the cottage he inherited, he is completely dependent upon his father. Do you really expect Sir Dalton Farrineau to approve his son's marriage to the daughter of a swindler?"

Although his words contained nothing she had not known before, they pained her. Shaken, she said, "I am very sorry if I have dashed your hopes, sir. By your laughter, you have repaid me in full." Suppressing tears, she ran down the path to meet Edward and Lucy. Then she turned back with them, and when they reached Sir Vale, he stopped Edward to ask, "My dear Mr. Farrineau, do you take snuff?"

Surprised, Edward paused. He wondered if Sir Vale meant to unveil a snuffbox amidst the larches and beeches. More than that, he wondered why Sir Vale should interrupt his tête-à-tête with Susanna to be polite to him. He resolved to find out.

THE YOUNG LADIES walked on, both looking back once or twice at the gentlemen. For a time, they walked in silence, except to note a noisy jay or a dog rose amongst the trees. It was Susanna who made the first effort to broach a subject of consequence, saying, "Sir Vale told me you have confided to him the truth about my father."

"Please do not be angry," Lucy begged. "I have never spoken of it to anyone else, I promise you, but I wished to see whether such information would cause him to cry off."

Susanna sighed. "It did not."

Lucy bit her lip. "No, it did not. I cannot tell you how it gratifies me to see that his character is so estimable."

"Edward does not esteem him," Susanna said. "He thinks Sir Vale is not to be trusted, and I wonder if perhaps he is right."

Troubled, Lucy nodded. "I know. Edward has told me of his reservations many times. That is why I had to see for myself whether there is anything at all noble in his sentiments and conduct."

"I suppose you consider his refusal to cry off as noble."

Lucy's eyes filled with tears. "I knew he could not be as bad as Edward said."

"I am certain Edward only meant to look out for my welfare by expressing his opinion of Sir Vale. He would not disparage the character of another man without excellent reason."

"Oh, I know. I do not blame Edward. I know that he had only your interest at heart. His affection for you is profound. Indeed, it is one of the aspects of his character I most admire. Oh, I wish it were not such a difficult matter to see you well settled, Susanna, for I am deeply fond of you, too."

This declaration made Susanna wish herself anywhere else in the world but at Blaise. Even living in Scotland would be preferable to hearing Lucy Bledsoe, of all people, speak of Edward's profound affection for her. The words grieved her inexpressibly, and she felt stifled.

Excusing herself in what she knew was the clumsiest manner, she ran down the path until she had put Lucy and the two gentlemen completely behind her.

"I SEND TO SHARROW for my mixture," said Sir Vale to Edward. "Perhaps you have heard of Wilson's Secret Recipe?"

"I have heard of it but never tried it," said Edward. He did not care for the effects of snuff, but he wished to hear what Sir Vale had on his mind.

"I keep my store in a very pretty box," said the baronet smoothly. "It is painted with the depiction of a castle, a splendid ruin which is part of my estate in Devon, and I can claim without fear of exaggeration that it is a genuine ruin and not a folly. I do not approve of follies."

"What did you wish to say to me?" Edward asked.

Sir Vale laughed. "So, you do not wish to dilate upon snuff in the middle of nowhere. You wish me to come to the point."

Edward smiled. "I have no objection to cordial conversation with you. We have no quarrel."

Sir Vale's smile glittered. "Well, as you are disposed to be cordial, sir, let me say that I have heard it said that you are a man of your word."

"I do not believe in giving my word merely in order to break it."

Withdrawing his handkerchief, the baronet waved it elegantly under his nostrils. "Excellent. Then I am glad I seized the opportunity that night in Sydney Gardens to enter into a bargain with you. You do recall our bargain, do you not?"

"Certainly I do," Edward answered. "I believe you agreed to make no proposals to Miss Marlowe for a month."

"Exactly, and you agreed not to speak against me or to put forward anyone else. You have not put forward anyone else, have you?"

"No, but I should like to know why you feel obliged to ask."

"Do you still mean to put no one else forward to Miss Marlowe? No one at all?"

"I said I would not and I will not. But I warn you not to take this as a mark of my approval. You are not the husband I would choose for Miss Marlowe. It is my belief, as well as my hope, that she will refuse you in two weeks' time without my saying a word or putting anyone else forward."

"But you have not changed your mind about our bargain?"

"Why should you think I have changed my mind?"

"I feared you might have found someone else to marry Miss Marlowe, someone whom you thought better suited to make her happy."

"You astonish me, sir. I had not heard that you were subject to fits of modesty, nor that you rated your charms below those of any man, living or dead."

Sir Vale smiled. "I am not, as you so acutely point out, a modest man. But Miss Marlowe is not in love with me. I thought perhaps you might have wished to see her marry someone she does love."

Edward regarded him gravely. "Miss Marlowe is not in love with anyone at all. If she were, I should surely know about it."

"Of course."

"Miss Marlowe's marriage is to be strictly a matter of convenience. Love will not enter into it."

"Then we understand one another perfectly," said Sir Vale. "I am not sorry to have stopped to exchange with you a word in regard to snuff. You are a worthy gentleman and will make Miss Bledsoe a fitting consort."

"Miss Bledsoe has refused me," said Edward.

"Yes, but she cannot hold out long against your proposals. She is a most amiable and elegant young woman and will soon recognize your excellent qualities. You are fortunate to have found one whose quality of mind and position in life are equal to your own. Lady Philpott informs me that your father approves the match wholeheartedly. You must let me know the instant I may wish you joy."

OUT OF BREATH from running, Susanna came to a secluded pond. She descended the stone steps leading to the water and contemplated the reflections of the cedars. In all the years she had had to endure punishments, slights and scandal, she had never repined, never felt sorry for herself, never told herself that things ought to be otherwise. But now, as she recalled the sound of Sir Vale's laughter, she did repine, did feel sorry for herself, did tell herself that things ought to have been otherwise. She wished the notion of her loving Edward were not so laughable. She wished the notion of his returning her feelings were not so absurd. She thought of Sir Vale's saying that "it would not do," and she wished with all her heart that it *would*.

Hearing a stirring in the trees, she looked up and waited expectantly. The sound was not repeated. Concluding that she had heard a rabbit or a hart, she picked up a stone and threw it into the pond, watching it make ever-widening circles in the water. Another sound in the greenery caused her to turn round. Then Edward appeared on the path and paused when he saw her.

Slowly, he came down the steps, concerned to see Susanna looking unhappy. "What is it?" he asked when he reached her.

She shook her head but did not speak.

He smiled. "Eventually you will have to tell me what is troubling you; I shall camp here until you do."

Looking into his dark eyes, she wished she could tell him everything.

"It is the business of your marriage, isn't it, Susanna? I know it must trouble you as it does me."

Bleakly, she said, "I am convinced I shall never marry, Edward."

"Of course you will marry, someday."

"I shall not, because I cannot do the things that women who marry are expected to do."

"I know full well you can do anything you set your mind to, even learning Latin. What is it you think you cannot do?"

"It is too appalling. You must ask Lady Philpott to explain, for she is the one who told me."

Laughing, he replied, "My aunt has her odd humours. You must not pay her any mind."

"Oh, but I must, for if her philosophy has any truth in it, then I am lost. More than that, Edward, I shall *want* to be lost."

Seeing that she was agitated, he forbore to tease. "Well, then, you'd better let me hear this philosophy. I feel certain we can find reasons why it ought not to distress you so."

"Reasons!" she said. "I am used to reasons. I have no difficulty with reasons. But I am not to be allowed my reasons." She turned eyes on him that brimmed with emotion, and he suddenly wished to be careful, delicate, soft, in whatever he next said to her.

"Let us say, Edward, that you and I are married—" here she blushed "—and let us say that I wish to spend a great deal of money."

His eyes went wide and it was all he could do to suppress his amusement. "You and I are married, are we? Well, I am sure you know, Mrs. Farrineau, that we cannot afford to be extravagant."

"Never mind that," she said. "I wish to have certain expensive items, and I am obliged as your wife to make you want them, too."

"I shall be glad to hear you out, my dear wife, but I warn you, it will do no good. We must live within our means."

"Please be quiet, Edward. I must think a moment and be sure I have this right." She soon became absorbed in searching her memory for Lady Philpott's exact words.

His eyes alight, Edward showed himself prepared to listen.

At last, she said, "Have you seen Sir Vale Saunders's new carriage?"

Edward did not understand why the subject had suddenly changed to Sir Vale, but at the mention of the name, he grew serious. "No," he answered.

"It is very pretty, painted yellow and trimmed with the blackest lacquered wood. It has lamps on all fours corners and seats six comfortably. The horses are black, too, and very handsome."

"Sir Vale is certainly wealthy," he remarked coldly.

"What makes the effect so delightful," she continued, "is the footmen. I have never seen such splendid livery."

Edward's expression became grim. He wondered if Sir Vale's wealth had made a greater impression on Susanna than he had anticipated. If so, then she was in more danger than he had allowed himself to admit.

"Indeed, I wish you had one like it," she said. "Surely you deserve one every bit as much as he does, nay, more, for you have genuine nobility on your side, Edward, while he has nothing but riches on his."

Hearing himself compared in such a light to Sir Vale, Edward searched her eyes. He found himself wanting to touch her. Before he could reach out, however, she began abruptly to pace. Earlier, he had been entranced by her grey-green eyes; now he was startled by the sight of her slender frame clad in a red spencer and red-feathered hat, moving back and forth in an hypnotic rhythm.

"It is appalling. It is every way horrible!" she was saying, her voice shaking with the accumulated emotion of the day. "Is this what I am to look forward to? Is this why I have put myself in your hands and the hands of Lady Philpott and Lucy, so that I may spend my life wheedling, and cajoling and lying in my teeth?"

He did not follow the drift of her questions. He only knew that this was a dazzling Susanna, a Susanna who had been so much a part of his life that he had scarcely noticed her before. But now, when they were out of doors, near the still water of the pond, surrounded by trees and sunshine as in days of old, her presence worked powerfully on him. It came home to him that if she married Sir Vale, he might as well lose a limb or be struck blind.

She moved to him and held out her hands. When he took them, she raised her eyes to his and said, "Don't you see, Edward? This is what I am supposed to do. This is what a woman is supposed to be. And I can neither do it nor be it!"

He pressed her hands to his chest. She was earnest to the point of tears, he saw, and he returned her gaze with intensity.

"If this is what a woman is and does," she continued, "then logically, I am not a woman, or at least not a very womanly woman. I suppose if reasoning and forthrightness belong to men, then I am more of a man than a woman!"

When he did not answer, she looked at him, terrified that he did not mean to dispute her last statement. She had opened her heart to him, trusting that he would reassure her. But he said nothing. As she waited in vain for him to speak, she felt oppressed, as though his silence confirmed her worst fears. Then suddenly, she felt the breath go from her as his arms went round her and he kissed her crushingly on the lips.

CHAPTER TEN

AFTERMATH

HER HANDS CARESSED his cheeks. His hands pressed her tightly against him, as though he meant to burn the sensation of her into his memory. He murmured into her hair and neck all that he felt.

Edward acknowledged now that he'd wanted to touch Susanna for an incalculable time. He could not place the hour or the minute when he'd first sensed the warmth of her presence, first desired to reach for her, but looking back, he saw that no matter how firmly he'd brushed the idea from his imagination, it had returned again and again. Sir Vale had read his feelings in his stares well before he had allowed himself to know his own heart. But now that he knew his heart, he meant to express it to the fullest, with the result that Susanna could hardly catch her breath.

Susanna, meanwhile, would have laughed and cried at once had her lips been free. However, occupied as they were, she could only give herself up to the power of the moment. After a time, Edward's urgent kisses quieted. He held her achingly, without moving. "Is it permissible to be so happy?" she whispered.

Holding her away, he regarded her. "Of course."

"But Lucy—what will happen to her? She will be heartbroken."

Edward smiled. "Perhaps she will not be as desolate as you may think," he said. "I have noticed that she is amazingly attentive to every word Sir Vale condescends to address to her."

With her hands on her hips, she stepped away. "Of course she will be desolate. She is the most sensible woman I know, and the only sensible thing to do in this case is to be desolate."

"Only you could imagine I could break a young woman's heart. You are too partial by half. I do have my faults, you know."

"You have no faults, at least none that I do not love."

He laughed. "Even my taste for reading Caesar?" he asked.

"There is much a wife has to suffer, I suppose."

"That is more of my aunt's philosophy, I suppose."

"My dearest Edward, you must speak to Lucy. I do not like having her on my conscience. I must give my full attention to resisting the impulse to burst out with effusions of joy. It is very ill-mannered of a lady to burst out with effusions of joy, unless there is no danger of her being caught at it."

Regaining his hold on her, he said, "I will speak to her."

"Now, my love," she said.

"Now?"

"What better time?" she whispered in his ear.

"You are very hard." Reluctantly, he let her go.

She watched as he climbed the steps, admiring his athletic grace and returning his parting look.

When he had gone, she inhaled, trying to absorb the reality of what had just passed. Ten minutes ago, the first wish of her heart had been too laughable, too absurd even to dream of. Now it was all true. Edward loved her. Amid his ardent kisses and yearning touches, there had been the words, spoken into her hair and her lips and her neck. Once Edward had set everything to rights with Lucy, she would have nothing to wish for. Her happiness would be complete, and every bit as real as the tiny caterpillar she saw crawling on the banks of the water.

"I believe I have you now," said a voice behind her.

Susanna turned to see Wilfred Sharpe emerge from a thick growth of laurel. His cherubic face wore the same sly expression it had worn formerly. He was exactly what he had always been, she thought with a sinking sensation.

As he came down the steps, smiling a little more with each degree of descent, Susanna's fists tightened. She had anticipated just such an eventuality. She had even asked Lady Philpott what she ought to do in this instance, and her ladyship had answered by speaking of new carriages and livery!

Suddenly Susanna recognized the feeling that had haunted her since the night in Sydney Gardens. What troubled her was not the thought of what Wilfred might say to tarnish her reputation in Bath. It was not *his* behaviour that concerned her, but her own. What she had feared all along was that he would do what he had always succeeded in doing, namely, goading her into doing something outrageous.

This time, she vowed, he would not induce her to behave badly. It was a promise she was determined to keep because so much was at stake. If she pushed Wilfred Sharpe into the pond, threw him in the brambles, or twisted his nose until he howled, she would never to able to forgive herself, never be able to say that she had left behind the hoyden of Cheedham, never be able to believe that she was worthy to be the wife of Edward Farrineau.

When he saw her quivering, his eyes gleamed. "I don't think I ever truly managed to frighten you before," he said. "You will not refuse me now."

She put out a hand to keep him at a distance.

"You were complaisant enough to give Edward Farrineau a kiss," he said in an insinuating tone.

"You will remember your manners, sir."

"I have no manners," he replied. Then, drawing near, he said, "I was most interested to see you kiss Mr. Farrineau." He tried to put his lips on hers but she moved her head, leaving him to kiss the air. Roughly, he pulled her by the arm. "I knew as soon as I saw you in the Gardens," he said, "that I should make you sorry. My only consolation in being sent to this vile place is that I've had a great deal of time to think of ways to make you sorry. You ought never to have called me that name."

"But *I* never called you Lily-livered Willy," she cried.

He let her go, leaving the marks of his fingers on her arm. "Then I shall make you sorry you ever heard the name."

She made as if to climb the steps.

Swiftly, he blocked her way. She would have gone up on the grass had he not shot at her, "I shall tell Sir Dalton about you and his son. He will put a stop to such goings-on, I warrant."

Trapped, she stared at him.

"Now, you will do exactly as I say, or I will tell Sir Dalton everything." He came close, sliding a hand along her arm. "First you will beg my forgiveness for all the abuse you have subjected me to in the past," he said, "and then you will beg me for a kiss."

Susanna closed her eyes. Her fingers itched to do what they had become accustomed to doing in Wilfred's case—defending her with all the energy at their command. But she must not slap his angelic face, she knew. She had resolved not to hurt him, and she was not going to let an insect like the young Mr. Sharpe shake that vow.

Swallowing hard, Susanna looked him in the eye and dipped in an elegant curtsey. In her most gracious voice, she said, "Lady Philpott must be wondering where I've disappeared to. You will excuse me, I'm sure." On that, she daintily removed her shoes, and in the most ladylike manner she could muster, waded across the pond.

LUCY COULD NOT FORBEAR asking Sir Vale why he was smiling.

The gentleman savoured his pleasure a moment before replying, "In a day or two, I shall renew my marriage proposal to Miss Marlowe, and I shall be accepted."

Lucy paled, then said, "Perhaps you are too hasty, Sir Vale. Mr. Farrineau will dissuade Miss Marlowe from accepting you."

"Oh, but you see I have Mr. Farrineau's promise to do no such thing. He has assured me he will not interfere at all—not for two weeks, at any rate."

"Oh." Miss Bledsoe put her hand to her forehead, murmuring, "But Miss Marlowe is not prepared to accept you at this time. She told me so."

Stopping on the path, he turned to her with a smile. "I shall convince her to have me. I have never failed to convince a woman I wished to have, and I shall not fail in this."

"Why on earth should you wish to marry a woman who must be convinced?" cried Lucy with emotion. "Would you not prefer one who loved you?"

He laughed. "Women in love are tiresome creatures. Miss Marlowe does not love me; therefore, I find her most interesting. I cannot recall when I have been so taken, so tantalized, so determined to have a female. Your sex, is, in general, too compliant, too disposed to please."

Lucy could hardly catch her breath. "You prefer a woman who does not love you? That is despicable."

Again he laughed. "You are entitled to your opinion, of course. I, however, find it enchanting. And if I may presume to offer you a piece of advice, it would do you no harm to take a page from Miss Marlowe's book. Her resistance is precisely what a lady ought to cultivate, and I heartily recommend it to you."

This hit caused Lucy's eyes to fill. "Miss Marlowe will never accept you. I am sure of it. All your wealth and charm will be insufficient to win her. She is not so blind to your character as some others have foolishly been."

"You are mistaken. When she learns that Mr. Farrineau refuses to speak against me, and when he fails to put someone else forward as a rival to my claims, then she will have me. Lady Philpott will see to it. Indeed, her ladyship said as much when she accepted some trinkets I thought to give her."

At that, he took Lucy by the shoulders and pressed his lips to hers. He held her until he had induced her to return his kiss. When he saw that he had aroused her passion, he pushed her from him and laughed. "You see my point," he said, "compliance and complaisance are the besetting weaknesses of your sex."

Perceiving that his kiss was meant to mortify her, Lucy wiped her gloved hand across her lips. "Until I loved you," she said softly, "I never had cause to feel ashamed. But now I despise myself almost as much as I despise you."

"You know very well you do not despise me," he replied.

"I had the devotion of a good man, a man of character, and I refused him. He would have loved me all my days. He would have kept me safe from such men as you."

"Perhaps it is not too late. Perhaps there is still time to accept the devotion of this paragon. He sounds a dull creature, to be sure, but what is dullness compared to safety?"

"I *will* accept him!" Lucy cried, hardly knowing what she said. "He will kiss me as a gentleman kisses a lady; he will drive you from my thoughts." She would have slapped his cynical, smiling face, but Edward came quickly towards them on the path, and begged a private word with Miss Bledsoe.

The baronet bowed, tipped his hat and went on his way.

When he had disappeared from view, Edward turned to Lucy and found her face streaming with tears. Alarmed, he asked what the matter was, to which she replied in anguish, "Oh, it is dreadful to love. One should do anything but fall in love."

Edward could not help smiling a little at this tragic declaration. "Are you in love, Lucy?" he inquired gently.

She looked up at him with large, wet brown eyes. "You know what it is to love, don't you Edward? You do not seek merely to amuse yourself."

"I believe you know me better than that."

"I ought to have known your character, but I was blind. Love blinded me. Thank heaven, I am no longer blind."

Although he had no idea to what she was referring, he offered congratulations on her miraculous recovery.

Suddenly she threw herself on his chest and wept bitter tears into his lapel. He allowed her to express her sobs until they subsided.

At last she asked, "Is it true? You have promised not to prevent Sir Vale's attentions to Miss Marlowe?"

"Did he tell you that?

"Yes."

"Do not distress yourself about Sir Vale," he said. "He will not trouble Susanna. I have seen to that." Then he held her away and insisted, "Lucy, what is this all about? You had best tell me everything. I will not leave this spot or permit you to leave it until you have told me what has overset you. I have never seen you like this."

Smiling through her tears, she said, "It is only this, Edward. I might have been married to you by now if I had simply heeded my own excellent advice on the subject of character."

Before he could reply, Sir Vale interrupted them. "You must come at once," the baronet said. Although his voice was steady, it failed to disguise his concern. "Miss Marlowe has had an accident. Mr. Sharpe saw it all. We must hurry. There is no time to lose."

SUSANNA APPROACHED Lady Philpott, who stood on the lawn not far from the main house, scowling at a rhododendron. Nearby stood Lord Blessington. He gasped when he saw Susanna's clinging wet hem, her soaked stockings and her teeth chattering as noisily as a woodpecker boring an oak. The day had turned chill, so that Susanna shivered in its increasing sharpness. When Lady Philpott looked up and saw her protégée in such a condition, she clapped her hands to her mouth, crying, "What has happened?"

"I do beg your pardon," Susanna whispered.

"You poor child. You will catch your death." She took Susanna's shoes from her.

"I was obliged to wade across the pond," Susanna began. She would have explained further but a sneezing fit interrupted.

"This is what comes of swoofing about to look at follies," declared her ladyship. She levelled a dark look at Blessington, and he wilted under it, for it said that if the poor girl should take a chill and die, it would all be his fault. Lady Philpott then dispatched her servant to the main house to see what could be done to assist the young lady. Although the owner was known to be away, his servants might afford them aid.

In a matter of minutes, the cook emerged from the rear of the house with a woollen blanket and, wrapping it round Susanna, hurried her into the kitchen. There the young lady was ordered to warm herself in front of the fire. Another blanket was supplied, and as soon as the unfortunate miss had been induced to drink a drop of the cook's own brandy, Lady Philpott bundled her into the carriage and set out immediately for Bath.

It was left to Lord Blessington to explain this sudden departure to the others. He waited impatiently, anxious to tell what he knew. At last Sir Vale and Mr. Farrineau came up with Miss Bledsoe. He availed himself of the opportunity to exclaim, "Here's a wonder! Miss Marlowe has been wading in the pond. I'm afraid she may have caught her death."

"What did you see?" Edward asked.

"I saw nothing," his lordship answered, "but I heard Miss Marlowe say that she had gone wading in the pond. I suppose it was an accident. It must have been an accident, mustn't it?"

At this revelation, the others rained questions on the young lord, none of which he could answer, but he soon discovered that he very much liked being asked questions and exciting amazement. Consequently, he favoured his listeners with a description of Susanna's bedraggled appearance. "Wet she was, through and through. Being a delicate female, she will perish, I should guess, before Lady Philpott can get her to a bed.''

As Edward's alarm grew, he turned to Sir Vale and urged him to drive back to town. Because the baronet wished to apprise himself at once of the state of Miss Marlowe's health, he readily agreed to this suggestion. Lucy, however, declined to ride with Sir Vale, declaring that she would wait with Lord Blessington for Mr. Sharpe. Therefore, Sir Vale and Edward set off alone.

No sooner had they raced away than Wilfred Sharpe appeared. He listened attentively to the report of Miss Marlowe's accident, then asked as many questions as yielded the information that his name had not been mentioned in the affair. A moment later, the three boarded Lord Blessington's curricle.

During the drive to Bath, his lordship experienced the pleasure of having Miss Bledsoe and Mr. Sharpe seek out his authoritative answers on the matter of the accident. He noted how closely they listened to him. Lord Blessington had not known until then that he had a flair for the dramatic telling of a story, and he was forced to conclude that he was a highly interesting fellow.

So delightful was the taste of this attention that he was inspired to relate the tale of the accident as soon as he reached Bath. When he found that he had returned to town early enough to seek out some of his acquaintance in the Lower Rooms, he discovered that, like his companions at Blaise, they hung on his words as he told the remarkable story. Moreover, on the following day, when he paid calls on Miss Murchen-Hill, Miss Hargreaves and the others who formed the multitude of his acquaintance, he found that they were all at home.

LADY PHILPOTT WOULD NOT ADMIT Sir Vale, Lucy or even Edward to the house that evening. Susanna had a fever and a chill, she barked at them, and they must run along and rue the day they ever permitted themselves to swoof off to such a place as Blaise Castle. When Edward returned to his lodgings in Milsom Street, he found his father waiting.

"I made excellent time on the road," the knight reported. "And I have not taken lodgings. I shall stay with you if you will have me." He smiled contentedly at his beloved heir. But his good cheer faded as soon as he noted Edward's drawn face and air of preoccupation. "What is it?" he asked in consternation, fearing that the young man had taken ill.

Too restless to sit, Edward paced in front of his father's chair. "It is Susanna—Miss Marlowe. She has had an accident, and I am not allowed to see her. I fear it must be very bad."

"Good heavens. I trust she will soon recover."

"I don't know how bad she is, Father. I cannot get any information. All I know is that she apparently fell into a pond at Blaise Castle."

Upon hearing this, Sir Dalton looked grim. Rising from the chair, he went to Edward and put a hand on his shoulder. "My boy," he said, "do you mean to say that Miss Marlowe has gone swimming again?"

Edward regarded his father in disbelief.

"And has she again implicated an innocent young man, as she did in your case?"

Edward's stare turned cold. "That is unkind," he said quietly. "I have never before known you to lack compassion."

"I beg your pardon," said Sir Dalton with a note of hurt in his voice. "I only meant to point out to you that this is not the first time Miss Marlowe has been discovered swimming and that it will, in all probability, not be the last."

"Susanna is very different now, Father. She is a lady."

The knight shook his head. "Miss Marlowe will never be my idea, or anyone's, of a lady. Nor should she be yours. Now, Miss Lucy Bledsoe, on the other hand! Why, there is a lady."

Stepping towards his father, Edward said deliberately, "I am not prepared to discuss Miss Bledsoe at this time."

Sir Dalton did what he could to rein in his temper. "You must propose to her again. You must not delay any longer. Do not mind if she refuses the first three or four times. That is to be expected in any elegant female worthy of regard. You must repeat your offer. Otherwise she will not believe you mean it."

"I cannot think of Lucy Bledsoe now, not while Miss Marlowe lies ill and I am not permitted to see her."

Sir Dalton watched his son pace. A premonition of doom now overcame him, and he stared at Edward. "Why should this girl's folly prevent you from asking Miss Bledsoe to marry you?"

Rubbing his temple, Edward turned to the fireplace.

"I know what has happened," declared the knight mournfully. "Miss Bledsoe resented your friendship with the Marlowe girl, as well she might. That chit is not fit company for either of you. Only such a featherhead as Mathilde Philpott could think otherwise."

"I must ask you not to speak against Miss Marlowe," Edward stated. "I am going to marry her."

Stunned, Sir Dalton tottered to his chair and lowered himself into it, too shocked to speak.

A painful silence followed. The younger man listened to the ticking of the clock, wondering if his father's implacability where Susanna was concerned might end by putting them permanently at loggerheads.

In his turn, the older man contemplated the bleakness of his remaining years on this wretched earth. He had been in Bath half a day and already his fondest hopes had been utterly blighted. And whom had he to thank for this calamitous state of affairs but Miss Susanna Marlowe? Not only had her father thrown away a goodly proportion of the Farrineau riches on a bubble of a scheme, but now the daughter had bewitched his only son.

Seeing what grief his news caused his father, Edward felt more deeply troubled than ever. He longed for the unblemished happiness of that afternoon, when he had kissed Susanna. Although that sweet embrace had been exchanged only a few hours before, he felt that he had aged much in the brief time that had elapsed since.

Sir Dalton turned his face away. "I shall not argue with you, Edward. Where you come by such obstinacy, I cannot imagine, but I shall not fire it up by opposing it."

Edward bowed his head.

The knight rose. "I shall go to the White Hart now."

The young man's head snapped up. "I thought you were to stay with me."

"I did wish to stay with you, but if you are to marry Miss Marlowe, I must remove at once."

Stepping closer, Edward said, "You will come to love her nearly as much as I do, Father. You will see how well she answers everything you ever wished for in a daughter."

"I do not wish to love her," said the knight stiffly. "I am content to despise her until the end of my days." On that, the old gentleman collected his hat and left his son's rooms, fully trusting that his parting words on the subject of Miss Marlowe had taught the boy a sound lesson.

LATER THAT NIGHT, Susanna's fever subsided. She was able to sit up in bed, propped against an assortment of pillows.

"My dear girl," Lady Philpott began, "I hope you will soon be well and about again, not only because I do not like to see you confined to your room, but also because there is a great deal of trouble and we must attend to it."

Susanna sneezed violently into a handkerchief. "You had best tell me the worst," she said.

"I am afraid the matter of the accident has got about. Wilfred Sharpe must have employed runners to spread the word. I could wring his neck! Catch me inviting him on any excursions ever again. The fellow ought to be whipped. If I were a gentleman, I should call him out."

Sighing, Susanna surveyed the carved mouldings on the ceiling. "Whatever needs to be done about Wilfred," she said, "I must do myself."

This declaration shocked Lady Philpott. "You are not well enough to give him the thrashing he deserves."

Her eyes glittering with purpose, Susanna said, "He has tormented me for too long. It is time I put a stop to it."

"Nonsense, you are not well enough to put a stop to anything. You are only just well enough to hear Sir Vale's proposal of marriage."

"Proposal of marriage?" repeated Susanna.

"Why, certainly," said her ladyship. "We must not waste time. What with word of the accident getting about, we must act quickly. I should not wish Sir Vale to be put off by idle talk."

"I am not well enough to see Sir Vale," Susanna interjected, "or to receive any proposals."

Lady Philpott's rouged face fell, but she bore up nobly, patting Susanna's hand and saying, "I daresay it is too soon yet. You look a fright."

Slowly, Susanna shook her head. "There is one visitor I should like to see tomorrow."

"Blessington?" Lady Philpott asked irritably. "I declare, I do not know if I shall ever let him in my house again, making us swoof nearly all the way to Bristol, and for what? For a folly!"

"It is not Lord Blessington I wish to see," Susanna said. "I should like Wilfred Sharpe to visit me tomorrow."

This request startled her ladyship. "That odious fellow, who repaid our kind notice by putting about vile rumours?"

"Yes," said Susanna with quiet firmness, "I cannot receive Sir Vale or anyone else until I have first seen Wilfred Sharpe."

WILFRED SHARPE WAS MANY THINGS, but no one had ever had cause to call him a dunce. Employing all his native shrewdness, he had assumed that Susanna would waste no time in telling her friends what had transpired at the pond, every last damning detail of it. Therefore, he had no sooner returned to Bath than he resigned his curacy, gave up his lodgings and was about to light out for Cheedham as fast as he could hire himself a mount, when he received a surprising summons to Sydney Place. He noted that the invitation betrayed no sign of anger or resentment, and he could not help wondering what its gracious style meant.

It had not occurred to Susanna to keep mum about Wilfred until the fever had broken and she could think clearheadedly. Before that, she'd nursed images of revenge in which Wilfred was alternately tarred and feathered and stretched out on a rack. Such punishment was no more than he deserved, she told herself; he'd subjected her to worse, much worse. When the heat of the sickness passed, however, she concluded that she was too weary of Wilfred Sharpe for such trifling satisfaction as revenge.

A plan slowly formed in her mind, a plan that called for her to have it out with young Mr. Sharpe once and for all. She wanted desperately to pull it off herself. Of late, too many people had been doing too much for her. It was time she took her fate into her own hands. But if she wanted to do this thing herself, she must keep mum about Wilfred's part in the accident.

Her resolve nearly deserted her when the curate was ushered into the sitting room. She watched as he was invited by Lady Philpott to sit near the sofa Susanna occupied. It took rigorous self-command to view the fellow's face with equanimity. After some minutes spent in conversation on indifferent subjects, Susanna begged her ladyship for a cup of her specially brewed tisane. The instant Lady Philpott left the room, Susanna said to the curate, "So, you are not content with sending me into the pond to flee your addresses. You must now set it about town that I went wading at Blaise."

She saw the young man's face go white. "I never said a word. I take my oath," he cried.

Susanna pushed herself up to stand before him and declared imperiously, "Mr. Sharpe, I demand that you desist from enmity this very minute. I remind you that you are a curate in the Church of England and that it is your duty to forgive those you imagine have transgressed against you." Here she sneezed.

Abashed, he sat back in his chair and looked up at her. She seemed to loom over him with a powerful force.

"Now, you will promise never again to behave in the ill-mannered fashion to which you have become accustomed," she demanded.

She waited in vain for a response. The most he could manage to do was shift about uncomfortably in his chair.

Leaning over so that her face came close to his, she demanded, "What is it you want from me, Mr. Sharpe? I know you cannot have been cruel to me all these years merely on account of a kiss."

"I do not know what I want," he said sullenly. "I only know that you humiliated me. You threw a lily at me, causing everyone to call me that dreadful name. You have always bested me."

Pursing her lips, Susanna thought for a moment before replying, "Then your object has been to humiliate me as you believe I humiliated you."

"I suppose so."

She stood tall and folded her arms. "And you thought a kiss would be the very thing to do the business."

"Yes."

She fixed him with her firmest stare. "Very well," she announced, "you may have your kiss."

"What?"

"You will kindly get it over with as quickly as possible." She looked him full in the face and pointed to her cheek. "Here," she said. "You will kiss me here and we will have done with it."

He gaped. Then, collecting himself, he said, "No."

"I said you may kiss me. Now get on with it."

"I certainly will *not* kiss you!"

Her eyes narrowed. "Did you not say that you meant to kiss me in order to mortify me as I have mortified you? Well, here is your opportunity, Mr. Sharpe. And here is my cheek."

"Never!" he exclaimed.

"What more do you require, pray?"

"I do not like your looking so content. You ought to look as though you were taking a spoonful of physic."

"I see. You would like it better if I were trembling in disgust and fear."

"Yes, I would. Damn, don't you see? You've spoilt it by agreeing to it. It hardly seems worth the trouble now."

"What is to be done then, sir? Must we go on tormenting one another for the rest of our days?"

Warily, Wilfred regarded her. "If I agree to desist from enmity," he said, "will you do something for me in return?"

"No, no, I shall not kiss you. When I offered, you hung back. It is too late now."

He shook his head. "What I wish is that you will believe me when I tell you I did not spread the report of the accident."

"Why should I believe you?"

Abruptly, he stood and cried out, "I don't mind taking the blame for what I did, but I'll be damned before I'll take the blame for Blessington. He was blabbing the story as we entered the city, stopping to tell everyone he saw on the street. As to myself, I said not a word. Why should I, when I know it can only end in your telling everything?"

At this outburst, Susanna smiled sedately. She returned to the sofa and with a sweeping gesture, reclined against a pillow. "Very well, I believe you," she said.

"You do?"

"Yes, I do." Delicately she suppressed a ladylike yawn. "This will serve as the beginning of a new understanding between us, Mr. Sharpe. Hereafter, you will conduct yourself like a proper gentleman in my presence. Do you understand?"

He nodded.

"In my turn, I will undertake never to douse, pummel or tweak you, nor do any other manner of harm to your person."

For a moment, he gazed at her. "But do you intend to tell the others why you went into the pond?" he asked.

She smiled demurely. "If I did tell, I fear the consequences would be very dire indeed. Such an unfortunate tale is certain to blight the future career of even the most devout clergyman. But I have no wish to tell anyone unless you force me to."

"Not me. I shall not force you. I believe I know my own interest well enough."

Extending her hand in a grand manner, Susanna said, "Then we have made a pact."

Wilfred approached her and wiped his palm on his coat before he took Susanna's hand. "Yes, I suppose we have made a pact," he said. Awed by her regal air, he raised her hand to his lips and took his leave. Thus, by forgoing one miserable little kiss, he saved his miserable little hide.

When she was certain he had gone, Susanna jumped up from the sofa, raised her skirts and danced a hornpipe.

CHAPTER ELEVEN

DESPERATE MEASURES

UNTIL HE COULD GAIN admittance in Sydney Place, Edward occupied his time by walking the circuses, streets and crescents of Bath. At last, gaining the top of Beechen Cliff, he looked out over the city and, for the first time in many weeks, saw clearly what he wanted and what he must do.

He would marry Susanna. That single act would provide her with the husband she required, the situation that would keep her from starving, the setting in which she would blossom and thrive. It would also provide him with the right, the inevitable, partner for his future days. Susanna, it was plain to see, was the only wife for him. In temperament, affection, intelligence, sense, character, warmth of feeling—in every way—she suited him; they suited each other.

Now he could see how blind he had been. Lucy had wept to him of her own blindness, and while he did not understand her reasons, he could certainly understand her emotion. His blindness had prolonged Susanna's heartache and apprehension. Moreover, it had caused him considerable discomfort every time Susanna's marriage prospects had been talked of. He regretted his blindness as much as Lucy regretted hers. But there was no looking to the past now. The future he had in view promised the most reasonable, the most natural, the most perfect end.

As he phrased a proposal of marriage in his mind, Edward noted how charming the city appeared under the fine, blue sky, and he would have smiled to think that he might make his offer to Susanna on this very spot had he not suddenly recalled that he had made a bargain with Sir Vale. That bargain, which had been intended to keep Sir Vale's courtship in check, now worked against him. He must remain mum on the subject of matrimony for an entire two weeks. For the space of a fortnight, he must suppress the first wish of his heart and evade all suggestions, allusions, and imaginings Susanna might put forth on the subject.

The idea of having to dissemble was as distasteful to Edward as was the idea of Susanna's marriage to anyone beside himself. A man of open, forthright and honourable inclinations, he had no notion of how to lie. Nor did he know how to tell the truth to Susanna without in some manner betraying the bargain—making a proposal by saying that he must not make one, asking for her hand by explaining why he was not at liberty to do so. Such truth-telling would constitute a breach of honour that Edward could not stomach.

Having recollected the bargain, Edward remembered the other obstacles to his marrying Susanna, namely, his father and Lucy. As to the latter, he had been sanguine in the hope that she would come round, that she would be far from devastated by his defection and might like to know that where Sir Vale was concerned, Susanna was no longer an object. But since their tearful meeting at Blaise, where she had sobbed into his coat and murmured incomprehensible references to his proposal of marriage, he could no longer say with certainty what response he might meet with if he withdrew his offer.

As to his father, Edward had even graver doubts. How could Sir Dalton suddenly regard as daughter-in-law the young woman he had been prepared to banish to Scotland? Edward was too fond of his father and too well acquainted with the old gentleman's disgust of scandal to demand any rapid turn-about.

He walked back to the centre of town while he mulled over these obstacles, and when he had achieved Milsom Street, he stood before his lodgings, deep in thought. How would he speak to Lucy? he asked himself over and over. How would he speak to Sir Dalton? How would he speak to Susanna?

When the answers did not present themselves, he entered his lodgings, and there he found a letter of such urgency that he was required to delay all other considerations.

IMMEDIATELY UPON READING the letter, Edward presented himself at his aunt's house, where he learned that Susanna was well enough to receive him. Her ladyship entertained the two young people with speculation as to the effect of the rumours that were rife in Bath concerning Susanna's accident. "I only hope Sir Vale will not cry off," she lamented. "He will not mind a hint of scandal, will he?" Then, in answer to her own question, she declared that such a gentleman could not help but cry off. "And then where will we be?" she demanded to know. "Am I to have the expense of the girl all my days? It is insupportable. She must have Sir Vale."

While Lady Philpott remained in the room, they talked only of the one subject, but as soon as she was called away, Edward sat close to Susanna. Achingly, she looked at his handsome face. He was tanned from the summer sun. His deep brown hair fell naturally in curls on his forehead. As he smiled at her, she admired his square jaw and expressive eyes. Even thoughts of poor Lucy's withered hopes could not mar her happiness. "Tell me what Lucy said when you spoke to her," Susanna asked.

"I have not yet spoken to Lucy."

"But why not?"

"When you sent me to her at Blaise, she was greatly distressed. I did not discover why, but I knew I should not say anything until she was more tranquil. Since then, I have been occupied with assuring myself that you were not going to die."

"People don't die of wading in a pond, my love," she said, stifling a sneeze. "But if you have not spoken to Lucy, how will we be married?"

Gravely he replied, "Let us not speak of marriage now. There will be time enough when I return."

"You are going away?" She searched his face anxiously.

"Yes. I'm afraid I must go to London."

"Oh, Edward. You cannot go, not now, not when Lady Philpott presses me to have Sir Vale."

He took her hand. "You know I would not leave you unless I had very important business."

"Edward, don't go, I beg you. What business can be more important than our marriage?"

She came close to him on the sofa and looked at him so earnestly that he wanted to kiss her. He resisted, however, saying, "You make it far too tempting to stay."

On that encouragement, she moved closer still.

Aware of her nearness, he did kiss her, sweetly and often. Then he released her, saying, "I should like nothing better than to linger here, but the sooner I leave, the sooner I shall come back." At this, he rose and walked to the door. Stopping in the entrance, he said, "I love you," and then, before Susanna could utter a protest, he was gone.

SUSANNA WAS IN SUCH LOW SPIRITS the next day that Lady Philpott granted her an outing. Her ladyship, at great personal sacrifice, accompanied her along the canal to view the waterfowl. When they returned to Sydney Place, they found that Lucy Bledsoe had come to visit. The ladies sat in the warmth of a sunny room, and Lucy congratulated Susanna on her restoration to good health.

"I suppose," Lady Philpott addressed Lucy querulously, "that your father has received a visit from Sir Dalton." When Lucy nodded, her ladyship complained, "Not once has my brother-in-law called on me since his arrival in Bath. He has neglected us abominably. It is dreadful to be dragged off to a sham castle and to hear poor Miss Marlowe's name whispered all over the town, but to be cut by one's own relation, too, why it is the outside of enough! It makes one feel quite low. Indeed, I am nearly as low as Miss Marlowe there."

"Perhaps my news will cheer you both," Lucy said. Looking down at her hands, she added, "I hope it will cheer everybody. It certainly cheers me." Here she flashed a stiff smile.

Susanna and Lady Philpott waited eagerly to hear.

"I have decided to accept Mr. Farrineau's proposal of marriage," Lucy said shakily. As she was unable to look Susanna squarely in the eye, she continued to gaze at her hands.

Lady Philpott clapped her hands in ecstasy. "How delightful!" she cried. "I cannot think of any two young people who are so well suited, excepting Miss Marlowe and Sir Vale."

Gravely, Lucy replied, "I believe Sir Vale means to make an offer to Miss Marlowe just as soon as she is well enough to receive him, and I understand that Mr. Farrineau intends to raise no objection."

Susanna, who had grown bloodlessly white upon hearing Lucy's announcement, now blushed. "I don't understand," she said. "When did you change your mind?"

"It happened at Blaise, just before we heard the news of your accident. You must forgive my saying nothing before this. Your poor health prevented me from speaking earlier. There has hardly been time or opportunity to be happy." Here she endeavoured to appear happy.

Susanna stood up and went to sit in the window seat. Despite the warmth of the sun, she shivered.

Keeping her eyes lowered, Lucy said, "Now that your marriage to Sir Vale is nearly a certainty, I think you will wish me well. I believe he means to try to make you a good husband, and if there is anyone who will make him into a man of character, it is you, Miss Marlowe, for he is terribly in love with you."

"You and Edward, engaged? It can't be true." Susanna said.

Lady Philpott felt obliged to apologize to Miss Bledsoe for this blatant contradiction. "The girl is not yet herself," she confided in a whisper.

Turning to look at Lucy, Susanna asked, "Did Edward tell you anything of what passed between us?"

"I have seen little of Mr. Farrineau. He has been called to London on a matter of business."

Bewildered, Susanna murmured, "This is impossible."

At these words, Lucy suddenly cried out, "Why do you think it impossible?" Her elegant frame trembled. "Is it so difficult for you to believe that I desire to be loved as you are loved? Is it not fitting that I should marry Ed-

ward, who has always acted honourably and loyally towards everyone who is dear to him? Surely you agree that
if anyone can be relied upon to cherish a wife and keep her
safe from harm it is Edward Farrineau.''

Her listeners gasped. Neither had ever seen Miss Bledsoe betray so much emotion. Susanna fell silent. She had
been as stunned by the news as by the astonishing manner
of its delivery.

Ashamed of her desperate outburst, Lucy wished now
to run from the house at once. Her escape was prevented,
however, by the arrival of Sir Vale, who was shown into the
room where the ladies sat and was pleased to greet them
with his customary insouciance. He could not stay, as he
was expected in Camden Place to dine with Sir Walter El-
liot. But he wished to know whether Miss Marlowe was
well enough to accept an invitation to an assembly at the
Guildhall the next evening. If it was not too soon after her
mishap at Blaise, he should be most happy to procure the
tickets.

Susanna was too shaken to attend to the invitation.

Lucy boldly interjected, ''I have just been telling her
ladyship and Miss Marlowe that I will accept Mr. Farrineau's proposal of marriage.''

For the first time since he had entered, he noticed Miss
Bledsoe. ''Please accept my best wishes,'' he said to her.
''And where is the groom? I should like to shake his hand.
Naturally, I must upbraid him for carrying off one of the
great beauties of the nation.''

Lucy hardly knew whether to fly out at the man or to
weep. Contriving to contain herself, however, she merely
looked away and did not reply.

''You are wise to select for your life's companion a
gentleman of character,'' Sir Vale said. ''Mr. Farrineau is
without equal in that province. Indeed, I quite depend on

his being a gentleman of character for he has made me promises of a most delicate nature. I only wish I could say I had as much character myself."

Colouring, Lucy replied unsteadily, "Mr. Farrineau is a man of honour, if that is what you mean."

"Yes, that is what I mean." Once again, he looked at Susanna. "Is this not joyous news?"

She gazed searchingly into his face. "Is it true that Mr. Farrineau has approved your addresses to me?"

After a thoughtful pause, he replied, "Why, yes, it is true. He vowed he would not come between us or try to separate us or sway you against me. Moreover, he has promised me that no one else will propose marriage to you. No one at all."

Susanna turned her head. "I see."

"Ah, you do not like our making agreements as to your future, and I heartily concur," he said. "It was officious in the highest degree, and if I had not been reduced to such measures, I should not have taken them. Desperate circumstances, however, call for desperate measures."

Stricken, Susanna could not lift her eyes.

Sir Vale found that Susanna in distress was as lovely a Susanna as he had ever seen, and he wondered how he might contrive to thank Lucy Bledsoe for getting Mr. Farrineau out of his way.

SHORTLY AFTER Sir Vale's departure, Lucy took hers, leaving Susanna to try to sort out the revelations of the afternoon. There were men, she knew, who thought nothing of marrying one woman while they loved another. Indeed, it was done all the time by gentlemen who transacted marriages in the same manner as they traded for horses. But Edward was not that sort of man. She could not be deceived in him. Despite her partiality to him, she believed that she knew what he was. He would not marry Lucy Bledsoe while he loved Susanna Marlowe.

At the same time, she could not deny that he had held off speaking to her of marriage, and it occurred to her that he might have manufactured an excuse to go to town. Perhaps he had repented of the declarations he had made to her. Perhaps he disapproved of her wading in the pond that had so lately been the scene of their tender kisses. Perhaps after such behaviour on her part, he could no longer regard her as the woman he wished to marry. Perhaps it was easier to leave her than to tell her.

She put her hands to her mouth to stifle a moan, angry at herself for permitting her feelings to be so open and undisciplined. It was her own hoydenish behaviour, her inability to conduct herself like a lady, that had brought them to this pass. She had no one to rebuke but herself.

"Are you weeping, my dear?" Lady Philpott asked.

Essaying a tiny smile, Susanna said, "I am only tired."

"In that case," said her ladyship solicitously, "you shall go to your bed. We do not want you tired tomorrow night. No, indeed, you must stand up with Sir Vale. You must charm him as he has never been charmed. And you must bring him to the point."

To HIS DISMAY, Sir Dalton found that he was acquainted with very few people in Bath. He strolled about the Pump Room, hoping to come upon a familiar face, but his luck was out. Wilfred Sharpe had returned to Cheedham, and Edward had gone to town. He might visit his sister-in-law; indeed, courtesy required that he do so. But even his knighthood could not compel him to visit a woman he disliked so heartily or to enter the precincts that housed the girl who separated him from his son.

With such gloomy thoughts did the knight approach the fountain of waters and take a cup. He was putting it to his lips when a voice stopped him. He heard: "She did, I tell you. Miss Marlowe waded into the pond. I saw her when she came out, and a sight she was!"

Inspecting the speaker, Sir Dalton discovered him to be a young gentleman whose nose dipped towards his chin. He listened closely as the gentleman said in answer to a question, "How should I know what caused her to do such a thing? I only know she provided much liveliness, which was sorely needed, for we had already been round the folly and there was nothing else to do."

Sir Dalton hovered near the speaker for a time, then made so bold as to introduce himself. Lord Blessington was delighted to find in Sir Dalton a fresh audience.

"Did you actually see the young lady jump into the pond?" the knight inquired.

"Jump? Surely she did not jump. It was an accident."

"I am persuaded it was no accident," Sir Dalton said. "Tell me, did she go into the pond alone or with a gentleman?"

Shocked, Blessington shot out of his chair. "I would swear she was perfectly alone!"

"I'm afraid she is accustomed to swimming with gentlemen," whispered the knight. "She has done it before."

Blessington froze. "I do not believe it."

"That is your privilege, of course, but you are welcome to ask the witness to a previous escapade, namely the Reverend Sharpe, Vicar of Cheedham, who discovered her in the water with a young man. If you write to him, he will corroborate what I say."

The young lord rubbed his pointy chin, musing, "I suppose you would not offer him by way of corroboration if he had not seen it. But I am amazed. Miss Marlowe, of all people!"

"You would not be amazed if you knew the facts of her parentage," the knight confided. "She is the daughter of a swindler."

This piece of news caused his lordship to recoil. He could hardly muster the patience to listen to Sir Dalton's history of Henry Marlowe, so eager was he to pay calls on his acquaintance and regale them with the latest titbits relating to the amazing Susanna Marlowe.

SUSANNA'S BALL GOWN was a soft green puff-sleeved sarcenet with a netted tunic of the same colour. Her gloves and slippers were white, as were the pearls she wore in her ears and the spray of flowers that adorned her hair. Seeing her protégée's serious expression, Lady Philpott exclaimed as Susanna descended the stairs, "Gracious, you look like a ghost."

Refusing all offers of rouge, Susanna at last agreed to wear her ladyship's sparkling emerald pendant. It dipped low on her bosom, riveting the eye hypnotically. Lady Philpott pronounced the effect perfect and predicted that Sir Vale would scarcely be able to contain himself in her presence.

They were ready in such good time that her ladyship took the opportunity to expostulate with Susanna on the importance of this evening's work. "We shall have numerous difficulties ahead of us," she said.

Susanna, who had her own difficulties to sort out, listened with a great appearance of docility.

"Our first difficulty is the gossip. You will, of course, be stared at as soon as you enter the assembly room."

This warning caused Susanna's eyes to narrow. "Let them stare," she told Lady Philpott.

"Exactly. But you will wish to give them something worth staring at."

Susanna's mind immediately conjured up suitable images. She would dance all her dances with Sir Vale. That would make them stare! She would reenact the scene at Blaise, showing one and all how it was that she had waded into the pond. Her eyes glowing, she asked her ladyship, "What do you think I ought to give them that is worth looking at?"

"You are well worth looking at just as you are, I daresay, and your figure has never appeared to such advantage, though I could wish you would allow me to add some colour to your cheeks. However, what is wanting is a certain air, an indescribable manner that the most elegant and fashionable ladies always seem to carry."

Susanna despaired. The sort of thing her ladyship had in view was not at all in her line.

"Let me see you walk," said Lady Philpott.

Standing, Susanna walked up and down the room several times before her ladyship cried out, "No, no, no. That is all wrong." She occupied the next fifteen minutes demonstrating to Susanna how she might walk so that her hips swayed in a flowing movement and she appeared to glide.

"That does not seem very ladylike to me," Susanna declared. "It is the walk of a flirt."

Lady Philpott smiled. "That is correct. You have a keen eye, I am glad to see."

"But a lady is not supposed to flirt, is she?"

"Of course she is, but she is expected to do it in such a fashion that no one notices, no one, that is, except the gentleman she is flirting with. Do you see?"

"I do not see. My idea of a lady has always been that she does not do anything that might be construed as seeking undue attention or favour. I have always thought that a true lady is like Lucy Bledsoe, whose manners are elegant and always calculated to make others feel at ease. I know that Mr. Farrineau thinks her the very model of elegance."

"My dear girl, that, of course, is the ideal, but no one really pays any mind to an ideal. In your case, a lady must draw attention to herself, at least from the gentlemen, and she must win their favour, especially Sir Vale's."

Here Susanna sighed. "I see. I am to be well-behaved and reserved where the world is concerned, but for the sake of the gentlemen, I am to be . . . to be what?"

"Alluring."

"I do not know how to be alluring, and I am sure you cannot teach me in a scarce few minutes."

"And I am sure I can." She then proceeded to show Susanna how to hold her net tunic wide in an irresistibly adorable manner. She did likewise with her fan, her left hand and her chin. "Now," said her ladyship in a whisper, "you must use your eyes. Those grey-green eyes of yours can be quite fetching if you manage them correctly. Watch me." Lady Philpott proceeded to roll her eyes, to blink and to stare until Susanna could not help but laugh.

"They will think I have caught a cinder in my eye or taken leave of my senses."

"The gentlemen will like it very well, I assure you."

"But what am I to say?" Susanna asked. "I have already asked everybody if they are pleased with Bath and if they have a large acquaintance here. I'm afraid I shall be silent and stupid."

"You must ask if they are pleased with the music, pleased with the dances and pleased with the company. Naturally, they will answer that they are pleased with you."

"You are too sanguine, I fear."

"Nonsense. You will do beautifully. Now what you must keep in mind is that if Sir Vale is going to hang back, you must see what Blessington has to say for himself."

"Lord Blessington?"

"Yes. You have noticed, no doubt, that he has not visited you, only left his card, which may indicate some reluctance on his part. I daresay the accident has put him off. The Blessingtons have never been renowned for possessing a great deal of backbone, but you may win him back if you walk as I have shown you, and if you speak and look as I have indicated."

"But why should I seek his regard if he is spineless and regards me as a scandal?"

"Because Sir Vale may disappoint us. I do not think he will. He seemed mighty pleased with you yesterday, but in case he does not make an offer, it will be well for us to have Blessington on hand."

"Lady Philpott, I should not like to speak with either gentleman until I have had an opportunity to speak with Mr. Farrineau."

Her ladyship's face hardened. "My nephew never has anything to say to the purpose except to make an objection. Now that he has given Sir Vale his approval, it is clear he means to make no difficulty. Therefore, it behooves you to bring Sir Vale to the point and give him your consent."

"But I must know what Mr. Farrineau has to say."

"It is clear what he will have to say. He will tell you that he is engaged to Miss Bledsoe and he will wish you very happy as the wife of a baronet. Besides, I do not believe that what he has to say will affect you nearly so much as what I have to say."

Hearing uncharacteristic hardness in the lady's voice, Susanna regarded her with curiosity.

"Aye, you look me in the eye, don't you, for you know what I am about to say, and it is this, my dear: because of that foolish accident of yours, it is all up with us. If you fail tonight, there is no looking for a husband in Bath. If you cannot win either Sir Vale or Blessington, it means that the gossip has gone too far and you shall have to quit the town."

"I am not afraid of gossip."

"Oh, but I am. I do not see why I should suffer because you were so heedless as to go wading in a frog pond. I do not mean to be hard on you, but you will recall that I had much to do to climb to my position in the world, and I do not intend to sacrifice it for you. You shall have to find your place in society tonight, for your place can no longer be with me."

Susanna could not fail to understand such a clear statement of the case. She therefore rose, permitted her mantle to be placed on her shoulders and awaited the arrival of Sir Vale to take them to the Guildhall.

CHAPTER TWELVE

PROPOSALS

AT THE HIGH STREET, the party entered the Guildhall, an unprepossessing building where a plain staircase led them to the magnificent banqueting room. The white walls, lined symmetrically with gold-painted columns at each entrance, caught the light of the chandeliers. The strains of a minuet sounded from the musicians' balcony. As Susanna admired the fine hall, she was not aware that the dancers had stopped dancing and the talkers had stopped talking. Quiet blanketed the room as every curl-framed face turned to stare.

A judiciously placed elbow in her rib directed Susanna's attention to the staring faces. Lady Philpott whispered in her protégée's ear, "You are not frightened, are you?"

"I have been stared at before," Susanna said steadily.

At that moment, Sir Vale drew near. "We are stared at," he observed.

Her ladyship deprecated the stares. "Fiddle! They have heard of poor Miss Marlowe's accident and think it a miracle that she is alive. They admire her endurance, as we all do."

He regarded the oglers, saying, "What lamentably tedious lives these creatures must lead to be forced to stare at us for their entertainment." Bowing low over Susanna's gloved hand for all the world to see, the baronet smiled. A murmur rose from the crowd. When the noise subsided, the gentleman said, "All of Bath is watching us, so that I will hardly have the opportunity to say to you what I wish to say. I think we had best dance. The others will soon grow weary of staring at us and will soon resume dancing too."

By dint of another poke in the ribs from Lady Philpott, Susanna was induced to be led onto the floor. The crowd parted as Sir Vale walked with Susanna. Lifting her chin high, she ignored the whispers and titters that drifted her way. She was determined to behave like a lady, and this time there was no pond and no Wilfred Sharpe to foil her good intentions.

The music signalled that the dance was to be the quadrille, which meant that the onlookers must give over staring and take their places. The intricacies of the figures did not permit conversation. However, Susanna could not meet Sir Vale's eyes without seeing them glint in admiration.

She had lain awake the night before trying to form a plan. The success of her meeting with Wilfred Sharpe had given her hope that she might be able a second time to take her fate into her own hands and bring about a happy conclusion. But her difficulties with Wilfred Sharpe had been nothing to this present predicament, for she could not speak to the party concerned. He was in London, and before he returned, it seemed, she was to be pushed and prodded into an engagement with Sir Vale.

In desperation, she sought a diversion. One soon presented itself in the persons of the Bledsoe family, to whom she waved gaily as soon as they entered the hall. When the dance ended, and the final bow and curtsey were performed, Susanna declared that she must greet her old friends. Smiling indulgently, Sir Vale followed her to a tall window, where the family stood.

Their walk towards the Bledsoes excited much notice and considerable remark. There were even those who turned their backs and let it be known that they meant to cut Miss Marlowe wherever she had the impudence to go. When Susanna glanced at Sir Vale, she saw that he regarded the snubs as amusing, and on this account, she began to feel a warmer sentiment towards him than she had felt before.

Laurence greeted Susanna with compassion for her recent illness. "It is wretched, I know, to feel unwell," he said.

"I hope you also know how it is to feel completely recovered," she replied.

"Indeed, I do. The Hetling Pump has worked its miracle on me. In fact, I may even go so far as to allow myself a dance. Would you do me the honour?"

Mr. Bledsoe stepped in here. "Is that wise?" he asked his son, rolling his eyes significantly.

"I assure you, Father, I feel perfectly well tonight."

"You will pay for it tomorrow, I fear," warned his father.

"Perhaps it will be worth it."

"Miss Marlowe does not wish to dance, I daresay. The gossip she excites must make her wish to be as inconspicuous as possible. You see, it is not merely your health I am thinking of, Laurence."

"I know very well what you are thinking of," said the young man. "You are thinking of my reputation." Putting out his arm, he invited Susanna to lay her hand upon it, and when she did, he led her down to the dance.

As Mr. Bledsoe looked worriedly after his son, Lucy stole a glance at Sir Vale and found him eyeing her with a smile. "I must thank you," he said, "for reconsidering Mr. Farrineau's offer of marriage. You have done me a great favour. I shall soon find the means of repaying such generosity."

Looking stonily ahead, Lucy said, "I do not accept him for your sake, but for my own. In him, I shall have a husband who is a man of honour."

"Unlike others one could name—myself, for example?"

"Yes."

"I should be happy to visit you after you are married. I believe we should find a great deal in common. You are a tolerable-looking woman, and I begin to see what others are pleased to praise in your elegance."

She stared at him, disbelieving.

"You need not pretend you do not take my meaning," he said. "I know very well what your feelings are for me. Let me assure you, it would not be impossible for me to return them in some degree. But for the sake of discretion, we ought not to begin until we are both safely married. Don't you agree?"

Lucy was afraid that she would weep if she tried to answer. She therefore went to her father, whispered a brief request in his ear and allowed him to take her home.

LAURENCE PROVED to be an excellent dancer. What he lacked in energy he compensated for in skill and grace. He and Susanna smiled at each other often as they performed their steps, and these smiles gave the young man the courage to suggest, when the dance ended, that they find themselves two chairs near Lady Philpott, where they might be at liberty to speak a few words in private before Sir Vale found them.

Delighted with this suggestion, Susanna readily accompanied the young man to a pair of chairs in a corner under a pair of full-length portraits of severe-looking guildsmen. Lady Philpott sat nearby, explaining to a lady in a red turban that once Miss Marlowe became Lady Saunders, those who cut her would be very sorry indeed.

When they had seated themselves, Susanna said, "Your father is right, you know. You ought to have a care for your reputation. Mine is as bad as it can possibly be, and therefore, to be seen dancing and talking with me will go very hard with you."

"I daresay if I were a young lady in your situation, I should be entirely overcome by the rumours. I should have to take to my bed for the rest of my days, or else go abroad."

"Then it is lucky you are not a young lady in my situation."

"Yes, I find that fact singularly convenient, for it puts me in a position to assist you."

Susanna looked at him in surprise. "I don't see how you can assist me."

"Lucy has told me that Sir Vale means to make you an offer and that Lady Philpott presses you to accept him. She also tells me that Mr. Farrineau has withdrawn his objections to your marriage to Sir Vale. I do not understand why he has made such an abominable aboutface. He knows what the baronet is as well as I do, and I depended on him to save you from him. But as he is not even here to make his own engagement public, let alone to protect you, we must look elsewhere."

"It is true? Edward and Lucy are engaged?"

"My sister tells me they will soon make an announcement. The engagement makes Farrineau careless of his obligations to you. Therefore, it is my duty to save you."

"I do not think I like being regarded as someone to be saved. I hope I am not so pitiful as that."

"If I put it in such terms, it was only to justify myself in my own eyes. I once told you that I would never marry, that I was too sickly a fellow to foist myself on a wife. Your difficulty has changed my mind. Perhaps I will not be so poor a bargain after all. Perhaps a sickly husband is better than a libertine."

"I believe you are proposing marriage to me, Mr. Bledsoe."

"Well, it appears I have not made such a muddle of the thing as I anticipated, for you understood my meaning."

"No, you did not make a muddle of it, and I thank you. You have always been among the kindest of my friends."

"Will you have me, then, Miss Marlowe?"

"I do not believe that pity is much of a foundation for marriage."

Abruptly, the young man stated, "I have made a muddle of it if you think I ask you only out of pity. From the moment I heard that you had thrown a lily pot at Wilfred Sharpe, I have admired you as I admire no other female. My regard for you has grown over the years, and especially during these past months, when I have come to know you as the most honest, lively and spirited young lady of my acquaintance."

Feeling her cheeks flush, Susanna replied, "I do not need to remind you that your father would not approve your marrying me. It would be best if you said nothing further about it."

"Am I to understand that you do not like me and will not have me?"

"You are more than kind to wish to assist me in this matter of Sir Vale, but I cannot accept you. It is true that I did not wish to marry him, but since Mr. Farrineau went to town, I have learned to think better of Sir Vale. He has been very much the gentleman where I am concerned. He has been gallant, indulgent and patient. Marriage to him would solve all my difficulties. I do not believe, therefore, that I am in need of being saved, and you may put your mind at ease."

"You do not understand. Saving you is the least of my motives. I believe that we should deal well together and that, in time, we should conceive a mutual and lasting affection for each other."

Rising, Susanna said warmly, "I would love you with all my heart, if I were not already in love with someone else."

She was spared the necessity of further explanation by the timely arrival of Lord Blessington, who, clicking his heels and nodding his head, congratulated Miss Marlowe on looking so well after her ordeal at Blaise. Laurence Bledsoe took his leave, and his lordship went on to say to her, "I inquired in Sydney Place as to how you did, and I did think to visit you, too, but I have been occupied with engagements of late."

"I am told," Susanna said quietly, "that you entertain your numerous acquaintance in Bath with the tale of my misfortune."

He laughed. "Indeed I do. They are most anxious to hear everything I can tell them, and I feel I owe you a debt of gratitude, for if I did not have the story of the accident to tell, my acquaintance would not extend me so many invitations."

"I am afraid the tale-telling has not had so blissful an effect on my own acquaintance, my Lord, for there are those who have cut me dead tonight and will not say so much as a word to me, let alone acknowledge me with a look."

Lord Blessington gasped. "Good Lord! Have I done that?"

"I am afraid you have."

"No, no. I gave it out as the most innocent of accidents—that is, I did so until I heard about the other swim."

"What other swim?"

"The swim you took with the gentleman."

"I did not swim with any gentleman. Wherever did you conceive such a notion?"

"Sir Dalton Farrineau mentioned it to me. He said you had swum with gentlemen before, but I assured him that at Blaise you swam perfectly alone. You did swim alone, did you not?"

"Sir Dalton?" Susanna asked. "Did he say who the gentleman was?"

"No, indeed."

"Did he happen to mention that I was a girl of thirteen at the time of the swim and that it, too, was an accident?"

"I do not believe he mentioned either of those facts."

Clenching her fists, Susanna scouted the room with her eyes. She thought she had seen Sir Dalton enter earlier, but in the crowd, she could not be certain. Now she looked for him purposefully and thought she spied him at the other end of the floor, speaking with Mr. Bledsoe.

Turning to Lord Blessington, she said hotly, "Do you see what has happened? By telling *you* the story of that old swim, Sir Dalton has told all of Bath." She shook her head desolately. "I did not think he hated me to such a degree. Now I see it is on my account that he neglects Lady Philpott."

His lordship peered sorrowfully at Susanna and said, "If I have been the means of broadcasting deplorable lies about you, I do apologize."

Hardly heeding him, she murmured, "I am not surprised that Edward has thought better of marrying me. He could not go against his father's wishes."

"If you wish to be angry with me, I shall not resent it, for you have every right, you know. Indeed, you ought to scold me soundly for permitting my tongue to wag as foolishly as it did."

"What did you say? Pardon me, I did not hear."

"I said you ought to be furious with me."

"I am not furious with you, my Lord." Here she sighed and wished she could summon the courage to approach Sir Dalton at this very moment.

"You are not furious with me?" his lordship asked.

"No."

"Oh, Miss Marlowe, you are the most forbearing young woman I have ever met. And you have the most conversation as well, for I never have so much to say as when I am either speaking with you or about you. Since I have had the privilege of making your acquaintance, there has been no lack of subject. Veritably, you have transformed my life!"

"And I'm afraid you have transformed mine."

Blushing red, he replied, "Well, I shall make it up to you. See here, Miss Marlowe, why don't we form an engagement? That would put a good many rumours to rest, would it not? Or at the very least, replace them with new rumours?"

"Are you speaking of engagement to be married?"

"Yes, I believe I am."

"This is most generous, my Lord, but it is going too far. You are not to blame for what has happened. Even if you had kept mum, word of the accident might have come out. The servants must have said something. You need not pay the rest of your life for a little idle talk."

"No, no, I have been indiscreet and I ought to pay for it. I wish to pay for it. Besides, now I've made the offer, I rather like the idea."

"But your family will not be at all pleased at your choice of bride. They surely have a union of a higher sort in view."

"They shall have to lump it if they don't like it. If I've ruined your reputation, it is my duty to salvage it."

Susanna could not help smiling. "This is too kind of you, but I cannot marry you merely because you believe you have an obligation to redeem my good name. It was never very good to begin with."

"Oh, but I should like to marry you. You asked me questions. No one else thinks to ask me questions, at least they didn't until I had the story of the accident to speak of, and no one else listens to me as you do. I should make an amiable husband, for I am prodigiously rich."

As his lordship completed this ardent speech, Susanna saw Sir Dalton bow to Laurence Bledsoe and move towards the centre door. Afraid he would leave the hall before she had a chance to speak to him, she made a hasty excuse to Lord Blessington and walked deliberately toward the father of the man she loved.

THE INSTANT he set eyes on her, he pressed his lips into a line of stone.

"Sir Dalton," Susanna greeted him.

He did not reply.

"I have you to thank, I understand, for the present rumours concerning my accident."

"I do not believe it was an accident."

Susanna flushed, for as she recollected the circumstances that had caused her to wade into the pond, she knew that the knight's suspicion was correct. Nevertheless, she persevered, saying, "I have always believed you were my friend. Even when you resolved to send me to Scotland, I did not think you did it out of malice but out of a sincere belief that it was for the best. Something has changed now, and I do not understand it. Why do you wish to see me ruined? Why do you wish to see me exiled from Bath as I have been exiled from my home?"

It was Sir Dalton's turn to flush. His character, ordinarily one of good nature and graciousness, now appeared to him in a very different and somewhat villainous light. He stood his ground, however. "You have come between myself and my son," he said.

Susanna looked away as she absorbed this news. She could scarcely believe that anything could come between the fond father and his excellent son. Moreover, it had never occurred to her that she could be the cause of such a breach. "I never meant to cause you and Mr. Farrineau to quarrel," she said.

"If you have any regard for my son, you will release him from whatever binds him to you. I beg you, do not bring him down, as your father brought down so many of his neighbours. Do not destroy him with your heedlessness, shamelessness and utter lack of all that is becoming in womankind."

Although Susanna was stung by these words, she was determined to have her say. Gossip, scorn and unwelcome proposals she could withstand, but she could not allow herself to be the cause of a break between Edward and his father. "Sir Dalton," she said, "you must make it up with your son."

"It is unthinkable. There are principles at stake."

"Principles are small comfort when you are lonely."

Wincing, he did not reply.

Susanna said earnestly, "It is more than two years now since my father left England, and I can hardly tell you how much I regret the time we have been apart. Do not, I beg you, insist on a separation that will bring you only pain and regret."

The knight regarded her seriously. "Tell me," he said with some gentleness, "how is it that you have never said a word of reproach against your father? He has destroyed your prospects and abandoned you. Yet you remain loyal."

"What would it serve to reproach him?"

"One does not ask what is served. One only knows what one has suffered."

"One knows that one misses those who are dear. You will miss your son, as surely as I miss my mother and father."

"You are a strange young woman. You do not reproach me any more than you reproach your father. Instead, you plead Edward's case."

"I love him," she said simply. "I wish to see him happy."

Sir Vale came up then to claim Susanna for the next dance. As she was led onto the floor, Sir Dalton followed her with his eyes. Could it be, he wondered, that he had been wrong? Was it possible that Henry Marlowe's daughter was possessed of a fine, unselfish and forgiving nature that rendered her parentage singularly unimportant? Was she perhaps not entirely unworthy to bear the name of Farrineau?

INSTEAD OF DANCING with her, Sir Vale stood apart with Susanna. "I will ask you for the last time," he said. "Will you accept my hand and heart in marriage?"

"No," Susanna answered.

"It does not matter to me that you love someone else."

Moved by gratitude, Susanna permitted him to take her hand. "You have been as steady a friend as any woman could wish. You have been everything that I ought to want in a husband."

Observing the glowing look on Susanna's face and the hand Sir Vale had appropriated, Lady Philpott now rushed to them, her arms outstretched so that she might crush her protégée to her bosom. "I wish you joy!" she cried tearfully. "I am sure everybody ought to be married and have a great deal of money."

"I thank you," said Sir Vale, "but your felicitations are premature."

Her ladyship's countenance went in an instant from rapture to horror. "You did not offer for Miss Marlowe?"

"I offered for her, but she has not accepted me."

Lady Philpott turned on Susanna. "You have not accepted, knowing how I feel, knowing what the circumstances are? I am shocked. I was shocked to hear of your being exiled to Scotland, shocked to hear of your swim and your other escapades, but nothing has shocked me as much as discovering that you disregard your own interest and have no notion of what is owed to me."

Susanna felt herself sinking. So often in her life she had given offence and disappointed those of whom she was most fond—Edward, her mother, Lucy, Sir Dalton and now Lady Philpott. Although she had known many difficult moments during the evening, never had she felt so oppressed. It seemed whichever way she went, she was fated to do and say the wrong thing. "I am truly sorry" was all she could manage to say.

"You shall look elsewhere for a means of paying your bills," her ladyship announced. "Sydney Place can no longer accommodate the object of scandal. You must remove tonight.''

Sir Vale offered his assistance, saying, ''I should be happy to find you a room at the White Hart, Miss Marlowe. It will, of course, look very bad, and it will be said that I am setting you up as my mistress, but we may make the best of it, and I should find such a rumour more pleasant than the general knowledge that you would not have me as a husband.''

Susanna reviewed her situation: she was to be turned out of doors to go she knew not where. She could not ask Lucy Bledsoe for help, for she could not bear to be beholden to Edward's betrothed. She might accept any of three proposals of marriage—to Laurence Bledsoe, Lord Blessington or Sir Vale. Or, she might present herself at the nearest almshouse and live on charity. Finally, there was the small chance that Mr. Sharpe's brother in Scotland still had need of a kitchen maid.

She gazed around her and saw that everyone in the room looked her way. Was there, she wondered, a general expectation that she would do something outlandish? Many of the expressions seemed to await it, even hope for it. The dancing had tired the crowd and something else was looked for in the way of amusement.

Defiantly, Susanna promised herself that she would do nothing to cause remark. Closing her eyes, she vowed that she would not break this promise as she had broken it before.

Then, opening her eyes, she saw Edward enter the room. He was dressed for travelling, not dancing, and an expression of relief crossed his countenance the moment he saw her. When he reached her side, he said, ''You must come with me, Susanna. I have something to tell you,'' and he led her out by the hand.

CHAPTER THIRTEEN

REUNITED

OUTSIDE THE GUILDHALL, Edward installed Susanna in a sedan chair, while he led the way on foot into the night's mist. In a few moments, they stopped in front of an inn. The door was opened, and Edward handed Susanna out. She was surprised to see that their destination had turned out to be the White Hart, but she did not question or doubt. Nor would she have questioned or doubted had Edward taken her to Cheedham, Scotland or even Blaise Folly.

The publican conducted them to a private parlour, where, when the door was opened, Susanna saw a grey-haired, darkly tanned gentleman still wearing his cloak and standing before a blazing fire. He looked up when she entered, and she stopped in the doorway. "Go inside," Edward said softly. "It is your father."

Henry Marlowe walked slowly towards his daughter until she ran into his arms. "My poor Susanna," he said over and over as he held her.

"You are trembling, Papa," she said. "You haven't caught fever, have you?"

He laughed. "No, I am merely cold. After the West Indies, I cannot get used to this infernal English climate. I daresay I should like it better if it were a trifle more infernal." He held her away and looked at her. "Good Lord!

You're a woman now, and a handsome one at that. I do not think I like your growing up so fast."

"Don't fret, Papa. I still fall into girlish scrapes."

"So Mr. Farrineau has told me."

Susanna sought Edward's face but did not find it anywhere. As soon as father and daughter had embraced, he had discreetly left the parlour to wait in one of the public rooms.

Walking arm in arm with Susanna, Mr. Marlowe said, "You resemble your mother, you know."

She looked down. "I wish I might have been a lady to please her," she said. "I'm afraid she despaired of me."

"You mistake the good woman, my girl. Your growing into a lady was the very thing she feared, for, to her way of thinking, a lady would be forced to shun such a mother as she was, one without birth or connections to recommend her."

"I thought she was disappointed in me."

"And she was afraid you were disappointed in her."

"It is a comfort to know that she did not despair of me when she died."

"It is a comfort to me that you were with her, for the knowledge that I abandoned you has weighed on me these past years."

For some time they remained silent, until Susanna thought to ask, "Will you be arrested?"

Laughing, he shook his head. "There was never any fraud. Your old father is not a thief, in spite of what's been said. It happens that investments go awry, as this one did, but a blunder is not a crime, nor is a gamble."

"But it's been said you would be arrested as soon as you set foot on English soil."

"Those who believed there was fraud would have endeavoured to have me arrested. But they would not wish to arrest a man who brings money to pay his investors. I believe I may persuade them to take back their blunt, along with all accrued interest."

"You have money, Papa?"

"Piles and piles of it, my girl."

"I am glad to hear it; I am in need of a bed for the night."

When her father pursued this hint, Susanna explained that Lady Philpott had demanded her removal from Sydney Place.

"She sounds an old dragon, and I shall certainly tell her so when I see her," said Mr. Marlowe. "But why should she quarrel with you? I am sure there never was a better-natured child than yourself. Have you fallen into mischief? Have you gone swimming in the Dance?"

"That and worse. Lady Philpott wished me to marry. She meant to get a husband to provide for me so that she should not have the trouble of franking my expenses. But I refused the gentleman she chose for me."

"Do you mean a gentleman offered for you?"

"Three of them did."

"I'll be damned. Well, they must be fine gentlemen if they have the sense to offer for you."

Smiling, Susanna rewarded him with a kiss on the brow.

"Well, never you mind marrying now. Your own papa is here with pounds a-plenty to keep you."

"Oh, but I wish to marry, Papa."

"If you really wish it, then I shall not object. Which of the three gentlemen is to carry off my little girl, then?"

"None of the three. There is someone else, and you must not ask any more questions until he asks me to marry him, which it does not seem likely he will."

"See here, puss. You say you have three who have asked and one who keeps mum. If you was my business partner and we was looking to turn a profit, I'd tell you to stick with the three sure ones and forget the other."

"But I love the other."

"In that case," said the fond parent, "you have my blessing to go and get him."

EDWARD WAS PERSUADED to take a late supper with Henry Marlowe and Susanna, during which time he explained how it was that he had been able to reunite the father and daughter. Ever since he had first gone to London in hopes of salvaging some of Marlowe's fortune for his wife and child, he had continued to correspond with the family's solicitor. Through this source he had learned that all Marlowe's monies were to go to creditors and nothing was to be allowed by the courts for the support of Mrs. Marlowe and Susanna. Through this source he had also sent inquiries to the West Indies to discover news of Henry Marlowe. Eventually, through this source he had learned of Henry Marlowe's return to England.

Having enjoyed a hearty meal of cold meat, fowl, fruit and cakes, Edward said, "I could not tell you the object of my business in London, Susanna, until I had seen your father. If he had been arrested, then it would have been my obligation to inform you of it and bring you to him. As it develops, I was able to bring him to you, and everything has fallen out better than I'd hoped. Best of all, you are no longer constrained to earn your bread by getting a husband."

Mr. Marlowe laughed, "From what I hear, the husbands would like nothing better than to be the means of earning her bread."

"What husbands?" Edward asked.

"Why the dozens and dozens who cannot propose marriage to her often enough, it seems," said the proud father.

"And if they offer for her when she is poor and a nobody, what will they do when they learn she is an heiress? No doubt they will have to make an appointment if they wish to make an offer, so many suitors does she have."

Edward did not take his eyes from Susanna.

"You must not mind Papa," she said. "He thinks it is his duty to puff up my attractions."

"Who proposed to you?" Edward asked.

"Laurence Bledsoe, Lord Blessington and Sir Vale."

"Sir Vale?" Angrily, he pushed his chair away and stood.

"You seem surprised," Susanna said. "I was told you expected him to propose."

"He gave his word that he would not propose for two weeks!"

Bewildered, Susanna said, "There must be some gross misunderstanding. Sir Vale is under the impression that you gave him your approval and that you assumed he would propose."

Edward put his hands on the table and leaned over to say, "I never gave him my approval. The bargain was that we would both keep mum for a month. I only made the bargain to gain time. I knew if there was time enough, something would turn up, and it has turned up, in the person of your father. But I never expected Sir Vale Saunders to go back on his word."

"Then you did not give your approval?"

"If you thought that, Susanna, then you wronged me." He walked to the hearth, where he watched the fire burn.

Susanna stood and said, "I am glad you did not give your approval."

Henry Marlowe looked from Edward Farrineau to his daughter and then back again. It struck him that these two young people had a great deal to say to each other, with

which his continued presence would interfere. He, therefore, excused himself on the pretext of procuring a bed for
his Susanna and crept out the door. He need not have gone
to the trouble of being quiet, for Susanna and Edward
would not have heeded any noise he made. Indeed, they
had long since stopped noticing him at all.

"It is a wonder," Edward said when the door closed,
"that I did not return to Bath to find you already married. I ought not to have trusted him. I knew he was not a
man to be trusted. What made me think his word might
mean something?"

Slowly, Susanna approached him. "It does not matter
about his word. If you could not trust him, you could trust
me. I did not accept him, any more than I have ever done."

He turned to look at her.

Coming closer, she said, "Thank you for bringing my
father here."

"I am nearly as glad to see him as you are, for now you
will not have to marry."

She paused. "I have not given up the idea of marrying."

"But you will not need to be in such a hurry about it.
You may settle yourself with your father and look about
you before you make any decision."

"I have already made my decision."

The intentness of her look caused him to pause. There
was nothing he would have liked better than to marry Susanna as soon as the banns could be posted. Nevertheless,
he felt obliged to hold back. Not for the world would he
hurry her into marriage. Not for the world would he have
her come to him with any doubts or confusion whatsoever. "Susanna," he said, "it has always been my wish that
you might be able to make as free a choice as possible and
not be forced to marry in order to live."

"Is that truly why you do not wish to marry me?"

He smiled. "I am well aware that the entire world has proposed to you, and that I must appear very odd in contrast. But I want you to consult your own wishes and only your own wishes. You must decide what is best for your future."

Susanna walked back to the table to think. Her logic told her that the restraint he advised was wise, just and honourable. The vicissitudes of recent days called now for calm, clear-headed thinking. The dispute with Sir Dalton required time to be resolved so that peace might be restored. Lady Philpott ought to be appeased, too, and a home found and furnished for Mr. Marlowe before there was any talk of brides and grooms.

Yet Susanna cared not a farthing for any of these things just now. What she wanted was to be Edward's wife. That wish had been uppermost in her mind and heart every minute as she had danced that evening. It had been as close to her as Lady Philpott's emerald gleaming against her breast. The wish to spend her life with Edward had been part of her ever since he had kissed her, ever since she had seen him that first night in the Upper Rooms, ever since he had danced with her at her debut, ever since he had smiled up at her as she hung from her tree reciting a paragraph he had taught her out of *The Gallic War*. Her love for Edward went as far back as girlhood, and she felt it too acutely to hold back any longer.

Moreover, she feared the event when next he saw his father and Lucy. She feared Sir Dalton would speak against her, and she did not rate her own charms so highly that she felt certain of his resistance to the elegant Miss Bledsoe's. Lucy was everything he had always wanted in a wife, everything any man would want in a wife.

As these thoughts raced through her mind, she began to pace. After a time, she glanced at Edward and saw that he observed her every move.

The instant Edward met her green-grey eyes, he began to think he had been hasty in urging her to wait before considering marriage. He knew that they belonged together. Why on earth should they delay? Why shouldn't he take her in his arms this minute and whisper into her neck? Why shouldn't he propose? Everyone else had, it seemed.

He would have held her to him then and there, but to his astonishment, she began to glide across the room.

She walked as Lady Philpott had shown her, allowing her hips to sway so that she produced a flowing affect. The silence in the parlour, the consciousness of Edward's eyes on her movements, the notion that she might have it in her power to get precisely what she wanted if only she could behave like a lady—all these sensations filled Susanna with electric excitement.

"What on earth are you doing?" he inquired at last.

"I am walking. Do you think I do it well?" Here she came close to him and turned her head so that he might have a glimpse of white shoulder.

He began to suspect that Susanna was flirting with him. Amusement now replaced astonishment, and he smiled as he said, "I don't believe I have ever seen anything quite like it before."

She now endeavoured to remember Lady Philpott's other pieces of advice. Recollecting what questions she had been told to put to a suitor, she began to despair. She could not ask Edward if he was pleased with the music; there was no music. For the same reason, she could not inquire whether he was pleased with the dances or the company. She sighed, wondering what to do next.

He watched her frown in thought. It was impossible to imagine what she would contrive next, but whatever it was, he was certain it would be outrageous, amusing and charming.

At last, she hit on the idea of holding her net tunic wide, in the adorable manner Lady Philpott had demonstrated. As Susanna walked, she took up the garment by the hem and flapped it in the air, making certain to wave her other hand gracefully under Edward's nose as she glided past. Glancing around, she saw with satisfaction that his eyes glowed.

It occurred to Susanna that she could not glide and wave her net tunic endlessly, for she feared that Edward would tire of watching her, though that did not seem likely from the tenderness of his expression. The arm she waved had begun to ache, however, and she now sought out her fan so that she might use it as her ladyship had prescribed. Locating it at last on a chair, she opened it so that it hid her face from view, leaving only her eyes to gaze at Edward through lowered lashes.

Noting that she was squinting furiously, he asked. "Are you getting sleepy, Susanna? Is it time for me to leave you? We may continue this highly interesting discussion in the morning, if you like."

"I never felt more awake," she said, coming towards him, keeping the fan raised. When she reached him, she stopped. Then, slowly, she lowered the fan so that it uncovered her nose, then her lips, her chin, her neck and finally, the emerald winking brilliantly on her breast. As she moved the fan, Edward's eyes followed it, and when at last they rested on the emerald, he moved a step closer to her.

It struck Susanna that it must look very odd for her to conduct herself in such a manner without some attempt at conversation. She had employed Lady Philpott's devices creditably; Edward's eyes confirmed that fact indisputably. But to bring him to the point, she must get him talking, and to that end, she looked up at him, rolled her eyes as Lady Philpott had instructed and said softly. "Mr. Farrineau, as you advise me not to think of marriage at present, you must tell me how I am to conduct myself in your company henceforth. I am sure it would not do to betray any sentiment that would give rise to an idea that we were engaged." Here she lifted her chin winningly, as Lady Philpott had indicated.

Containing his laughter, he replied, "I imagine that you will conduct yourself as you always do, Susanna."

"And what way is that?" she murmured.

"Unpredictably."

"Are you laughing at me?"

"No. But I cannot help observing that you do not stand still a minute and that you blink your eyes a great deal."

Although she was not certain that his reply constituted a compliment, she thought it to her advantage to treat it as one. After making a graceful curtsey, she approached him so that her face was very close to his. Boldly she said, "Until you see fit to ask me to marry you, I suppose I shall have to speak to you of inconsequentials, as though you and I were strangers."

He availed himself of the opportunity to inhale her scent. "And I shall have to address you as Miss Marlowe and pretend I am not amused by your escapades."

"Tell me, Mr. Farrineau," she said lightly, "are you pleased with Bath?"

"Indeed, Miss Marlowe, at this moment, it is very nearly paradise."

"And do you have a large acquaintance in Bath?" Here she waved her fan so that a breath of cool air fell on them both.

Without taking his eyes from hers, he stopped the fan with his hand. She was, he acknowledged, the most outrageous woman he had ever beheld, and wholly irresistible. His hand slid from the fan along her arm to her shoulder and neck, and when it came to her chin, he tilted her face so that her lips were raised to his. Susanna closed her eyes expectantly. She kept them closed for a time, but when she felt nothing, she opened them wide.

She found him studying her. Although his former scruples had been laid to rest, he found it impossible to resist smiling at her dazzling display of coquetry.

She stepped away, a little daunted by his failure to kiss her, a little frightened that perhaps she had made a fool of herself.

Suddenly she felt his hand on her waist. In another moment, his arms were around her, holding her to him. He kissed her with such power that she could not breathe. The force of his embrace assured her that his earlier resistance had not been caused by any lack of desire, and she rejoiced, clinging to his lips and touching her fingers to his face.

He released her as abruptly as he had seized her, and, unsteadily, she stepped back against the wall. She breathed hard and saw that his eyes caressed every inch of her. In answer to his look, she spoke his name, and he came to her, holding her cheeks and pressing himself to her with searching lips. "Will you marry me?" he said in her ear, kissing it.

She felt a joyous laugh start, then stick like a fist in her throat. Having just received all the proofs of affection she had desired, she ought now to have savoured glorious triumph. She did not, however. On the contrary, she felt somewhat nauseated.

Into her mind came an image of herself as she must have appeared to Edward, with one hand sawing the air and the other flapping her net tunic. Her artful ways with the fan came back to her, as did her sundry attempts to be what Lady Philpott referred to as "alluring." The images overcame her with revulsion. She wished she had never heard of any devices; she wished she had never thought to employ them; she wished she had not used them as weapons against Edward.

Throughout her life, Susanna had never looked back with such regret as she did now. No scrape, no folly, no unladylike misstep had ever caused her such shame as did her late conduct. She had schemed. She had seduced. She had played falsely with the man she adored.

Who had Edward proposed to, she asked herself. It was not the Susanna Marlowe he had known all these years. It was a coquette who had campaigned to extort a proposal of marriage from him, completely disregarding his reservations. She had set out to : ud his reason and play on his tenderness for her, and she had succeeded. She did not recognize this artful creature—this creature who was now an accomplished lady.

What would happen the next time she wished to extort something from Edward? Would she resurrect that alluring female, even though it made her ill to do so? Would she go on pretending to be that "lady" over and over again, for the rest of her life? The temptation would be great, especially as she had met with such success on the first trial. On the other hand, she could no more stomach such a pretence than she could transform herself into Lucy Bledsoe.

Anguished, she pushed Edward from her. To marry him now would be to feel sick at heart for the rest of her life. She might be a scandal, a mischief-maker and a hoyden hopeless of remedy, but until tonight, she had never been a cheat.

"You have not forgotten the question, I hope," he said. Then, seeing the emotion on her face, he stepped closer to say, "Susanna, you do wish to marry me, don't you?"

And because she could not deny it, she said nothing as she ran from the room.

CHAPTER FOURTEEN

FURTHER LESSONS

WHEN EDWARD ENTERED his lodgings, he found Sir Dalton awaiting his return. "Is it true, my boy?" the knight cried. "Has Henry Marlowe returned to England? The town is buzzing with the news. It is said that he has returned to make it up to his investors. Can it be true?"

Edward nodded. "Yes, Mr. Marlowe has come back, and with ample funds to repay his investors."

Sir Dalton would have clapped his hands with joy, but seeing the grim expression on his son's face, he placed an affectionate hand on his shoulder. "Do not distress yourself," he said. "I remove my objections to your marrying Miss Marlowe."

Bleakly, Edward gazed at his father.

"There, there! All is well again, I assure you. It is not merely on her father's account that I have changed my mind, though that is certainly an inducement and I shall not object to having my money again. But tonight I learned that Miss Marlowe is a most generous young woman. She might easily have borne me a grudge and done what she could to turn you irrevocably against me. Instead, she did her utmost to heal the breach between us. She hasn't a rancorous bone in her body, and I found I could not help liking her. Therefore, you may stop frowning and go to your lady love."

"I have just come from her," Edward said quietly.

"Excellent. When next you see her, you may say that I am resolved to make a handsome marriage settlement on you both. I am prepared to give exactly what Marlowe gives you, as soon as I am paid what he owes me."

"I am glad you like Susanna now, Father, but talk of settlements is unwarranted, I fear."

"Perhaps I ought to go to her and explain that I have had a change of heart since we last spoke. I'm afraid I left her with the impression that I rather disapprove of her. Then, after I have spoken my piece, you may propose to her."

"I did propose to her, Father, and she did not accept."

In disbelief the knight cried, "But she loves you to distraction. She told me so. She is a very outspoken young woman, you know."

Edward said passionately, "I don't understand it. One moment she was doing everything in her power to captivate me; the next, she was running from me as though I were an ogre."

Sir Dalton sighed and sank into a chair. "I know she loves you. She could not have said what she said to me and not love you. Indeed, her honest declaration of love gave me the first inkling that I had done her an injustice. It is living with Lady Philpott that has done this to her! That harridan has addled the poor girl's brain. Gad, Edward, what the deuce are we going to do now?"

"I will not be driven off, I can tell you that."

Anxiously, the father watched his son pace.

"She cannot wave her fan at me and walk up and down in front of me and drive me quite wild and then not accept me," Edward declared. "To refuse to marry me after such carryings-on is tantamount to a breach of promise."

"Good Lord. You do not mean to go to court, do you?"

For the first time since his return, Edward laughed. "No, Father. I mean to go to bed. We have much to do in the morning."

"I shall do anything I can to help, my boy."

"Excellent. You may visit Lady Philpott."

"What? Edward, I know it was very bad of me to have disliked the girl so much all these years, but this is hard punishment indeed!"

"While you are marshalling her ladyship to our noble cause," Edward continued, "I shall have a talk with Miss Lucy Bledsoe."

On this, the young man bade his father good-night. As Sir Dalton sat back in his chair to contemplate the odd reversal of recent events, he resigned himself to paying a call on his sister-in-law.

HENRY MARLOWE was standing in the hall outside Susanna's door, begging her to speak to him, for pity's sake, when Edward arrived with Sir Dalton, Lady Philpott and Lucy Bledsoe in tow. As soon as introductions and greetings had passed all round, Edward took himself off to the private parlour below stairs.

Her ladyship then threw her shoulders back and set to pounding on Susanna's door. "It is I, Lady Philpott, dear girl. I've come to say that I no longer insist upon your marrying Sir Vale. I should never have been so insistent if I had known that Edward wished to have you. I shall be happy to welcome you again in Sydney Place, and your father, too, but first you must come out of your room."

Susanna opened the door a crack.

Seizing her hand, her ladyship crowed, "I knew I should be the one to persuade you to come out of hiding."

Susanna smiled sadly. "I wish to say how sorry I am that we quarrelled, my Lady."

"Never mind all that. You must hear my nephew out. He is worth a hundred Sir Vales, and when Dalty came to me and told me of this pickle of yours, I vowed you should have him. If Dalty makes you any trouble, you may come to me, and I shall set him to rights in short order." Here she shot a warning look at her brother-in-law.

"It is you who have made trouble, letting the poor child fall into a pond!" the knight retorted hotly. Then, with a gentle smile, he turned to Susanna to say, "In truth, Miss Marlowe, I do not wish to stand between you and Edward. I know you are too generous to refuse to hear my son out. Hear him with his father's blessing."

Susanna's eyes brimmed at this softness, and she opened the door wide.

Then Lucy took Susanna's hand and drew her into the corridor. "Susanna, I bring you a letter from my brother."

With difficulty, Susanna glanced at Lucy, who smiled warmly and pressed the letter into her hand. Opening it, Susanna read:

My dear Miss Marlowe,
Mr. Farrineau has explained the reason for his sudden journey to town, and I am satisfied. The gentleman clearly regards you with a healthy, energetic and most sincere affection, and I hope you will not think me fickle if I now withdraw my offer of marriage. It will give me pleasure to know that as Mrs. Farrineau, you will be free to honeymoon as far from the Hetling Pump as it is possible to get. Please accept my very best wishes for your good health and happiness.
Yours, etc.,
Laurence Bledsoe

When Susanna had finished reading, Lucy laid a hand on her arm and said, "I want you to know that you are free to marry Edward. I do not wish to stand in your way, I promise.''

Susanna shook her head.

Earnestly, Lucy reassured her. "When he came to me this morning, I was obliged to confess to him what I now confess to you, my dear: I did not mean it when I said I would accept him. It was despair that prompted me to say such a spiteful thing. I found myself in love with Sir Vale, against my will, against my judgement. Somehow I had contrived to form an attachment to a man whose character I could not admire, whose honour I could not trust. For a time, I clung to the hope that Edward would save me from myself. But now I do not wish to have Edward save me. Indeed, I have saved myself, as it was right that I should do. Now I must know that you forgive me. I will not rest until I see you and Edward reconciled.''

Susanna replied, "How dreadful it must have been for you to hear of Sir Vale's relentless proposals to me. I am sorry if I caused you any pain, Lucy. Indeed, I never meant to.''

Here the two young women embraced and sniffled and dabbed their eyes with their linens until Lucy said, "You must go and tell Edward you will marry him. He is waiting for you in the private parlour just below.''

"I cannot do that," Susanna stated solemnly. "Edward and I can never marry.''

Lucy and the others looked at one another. Henry Marlowe sighed and said, "Susanna, puss, do you not think your mama would like you to accept the man who gave her Larkwhistle Cottage?''

"She would like it above all things," Susanna replied, "but it cannot be.''

"What are we to do?'' the father asked helplessly.

After a moment, Susanna said, "You have all been very kind and have done what you could, but the fact is, it is up to me to do something. I once vowed never again to quarrel with Edward, and I mean to keep that vow. I will go to him and explain why we must part."

As soon as she had taken leave of them and disappeared down the stairs, Lady Philpott turned to Lucy to observe, "It really is too bad you don't fancy Sir Vale any longer. He is entirely at liberty at the moment."

Lucy laughed. "I wish him joy of his liberty, for I fully intend to have joy of mine."

"But now I think of it," her ladyship continued, "a young lady of your beauty and manners may surely do better than a baronet. In fact, I have heard that the Marquess of Cleeve has lately arrived in Bath. He is worth ten thousand a year if he's worth a groat, which is somewhat less than Sir Vale, but still, to be a marchioness! Now, my dear, that is my idea of mending a broken heart!"

EDWARD ROSE FROM HIS CHAIR the instant Susanna entered the parlour. She studied to avoid his eyes but could not escape the consciousness of his presence.

"I believe I ought to explain," she began. She looked up to see him regarding her intensely. "We have always talked, have we not, Edward? And it is fitting that I should tell you the truth. You deserve no less than the truth."

"Very well. I should like to hear some explanation for last night." He sat down in his chair and waited.

She took the chair opposite his. Drawing a deep breath, she fixed her eye on a point in space and said, "I extorted that proposal of marriage from you. You did not wish to make it, but I got it out of you anyway."

He came to her and took her hand. "Susanna, why did you run away from me?"

"I cannot tell you while you are holding me. I cannot think."

He withdrew and resumed his seat.

Without looking at him, she said, "I ran away because I employed various arts against you, arts which form the arsenal of every lady, I am told, but which I had never before employed against anyone, will never again employ against anyone, and which I am heartily ashamed to have employed against you."

He would have come to her again but thought better of it. "Arts? What arts?" he asked.

She coloured deeply. "Perhaps you recall that I walked."

He smiled at the recollection. "I do recall. It was unforgettable. I have never seen such walking."

"There! That is what I mean! But not only did I walk, I used my fan against you, and not only my fan, but my tunic, and my hand, and everything Lady Philpott said a lady ought to use."

"I wondered where you had come by such devices. You certainly did not get them out of *The Gallic War*."

Despite the gentle amusement in his voice, she would not meet his eyes. "Don't you see, I did exactly what I have always insisted was perfectly appalling. I did what I had vowed never to do. I treated you as a puppet, to be used and manipulated. I swore I would not be a wife whose principal employment consisted in making her husband do what he had no intention of doing, and yet that is what I was on the verge of becoming."

He regarded her fine profile, a profile that was so familiar, so dear to him that he knew every inch of it by heart. "Do you think I proposed marriage to you because you drove me to it, because your arts drove me to it?"

She bowed her head. "I was alluring. You could not help yourself."

"I do not know how to say this in such a way as to spare your feelings, my love, for you were very alluring indeed, but not because you employed your arts so well. You were alluring because you employed them so badly."

She looked up at him. "Badly! I did everything exactly as Lady Philpott prescribed. I inflamed you, did I not?"

"Oh, yes, you did that."

She endeavoured to ignore the power in his voice. "And you proposed marriage, did you not?"

"Yes, but not because you worked your arts against me."

"Then why?"

He sat back, folding his arms, appraising her with a tender expression. "Because you were irresistible, marching up and down in that ridiculous fashion, and I thought I should be a fool to put off marrying a woman who would go to such trouble to get me."

Susanna was stunned. "I thought I had bewitched you."

"You did. You do." He came and knelt before her. Taking her hand, he opened it so that he might look into her palm. Then he kissed it.

"This is mere pity," she said unsteadily. "And I know whence it comes. It seems I am ridiculous no matter what I do, whether it is falling out of trees, wading into ponds or beguiling gentlemen with my feminine arts."

This time he would not permit her to evade his look. Lifting his hands to her face, he said, "I am sensible of many things when I look at you, Susanna, but not one of them resembles pity."

Whereas a moment before, she could not so much as glance at him, now she could not wrench her eyes away. "I wished so much to be a lady," she murmured.

"You *are* a lady. You are kind and good-hearted and honest and brave. You need never be more of a lady than that. You need never be other than what you are, for what you are is delicious. I might also add, you are never dull."

"But everyone was so determined to teach me to be a lady," she said with a sigh.

Standing, he pulled her to her feet, saying, "If you will permit me, I will undertake to teach you one more lesson—that you are loved."

Closing her eyes, she threw her arms around him. He lifted a wisp of curl from her neck and brushed his lips against the bare skin. She felt the warmth of his breath as he said, "Marry me, Susanna."

When at last her lips were sufficiently free to permit her to answer, she declared that she would certainly marry him at the earliest possible date, for he had unfolded to her a subject to which she wished to devote a lifetime of study.

Harlequin Regency Romance™

COMING NEXT MONTH

#23 PRESCOTT'S LADY by Clarice Peters
Lady Eleanor Whiting and Lord Peter Prescott had
been engaged until Eleanor discovered that Peter had
not given up the mistress he had promised he would.
True to form, Eleanor returned his engagement ring in
a bit o'muslin and created a public scandal that made
Peter the laughingstock of the ton. When
circumstances throw them together three years later,
the legendary battle begins anew, but this time the
battle concludes with a turn of events that surprises
them both!

#24 LORD TOM by Patricia Wynn
When Lord Tom Harleston promised Susan
Johnstone's father to get her safely back to England,
he was already half in love. Although Susan was
reluctant to risk Tom's reputation on such a
dangerous adventure, she succumbed to his
enthusiasm and twinkling brown eyes. But once
back in England, another adventure began. One that
could reveal their true identities and send Susan to
the gallows....

In April, Harlequin brings you the
world's most popular romance author

JANET DAILEY

No Quarter Asked

Out of print since 1974!

After the tragic death of her father, Stacy's world is shattered. She needs to get away by herself to sort things out. She leaves behind her boyfriend, Carter Price, who wants to marry her. However, as soon as she arrives at her rented cabin in Texas, Cord Harris, owner of a large ranch, seems determined to get her to leave. When Stacy has a fall and is injured, Cord reluctantly takes her to his own ranch. Unknown to Stacy, Carter's father has written to Cord and asked him to keep an eye on Stacy and try to convince her to return home. After a few weeks there, in spite of Cord's hateful treatment that involves her working as a ranch hand and the return of Lydia, his ex-fiancée, by the time Carter comes to escort her back, Stacy knows that she is in love with Cord and doesn't want to go.

**Watch for *Fiesta San Antonio* in July and
For Bitter or Worse in September.**

JDA-1

You'll flip . . . your pages won't!
Read paperbacks *hands-free* with

Book Mate • I

The perfect "mate" for all your romance paperbacks
Traveling • Vacationing • At Work • In Bed • Studying
• Cooking • Eating

Perfect size for all standard paperbacks, this wonderful invention makes reading a pure pleasure! Ingenious design holds paperback books OPEN and FLAT so even wind can't ruffle pages — leaves your hands free to do other things. Reinforced, wipe-clean vinyl-covered holder flexes to let you turn pages without undoing the strap . . . supports paperbacks so well, they have the strength of hardcovers!

Pages turn WITHOUT opening the strap.

SEE-THROUGH STRAP

Reinforced back stays flat.

Built in bookmark

BOOK MARK

BACK COVER
HOLDING STRIP

10" x 7¼". opened.
Snaps closed for easy carrying, too.

Available now. Send your name, address, and zip code, along with a check or money order for just $5.95 + .75¢ for postage & handling (for a total of $6.70) payable to Reader Service to:

Reader Service
Bookmate Offer
901 Fuhrmann Blvd.
P.O. Box 1396
Buffalo, N.Y. 14269-1396

Offer not available in Canada
*New York and Iowa residents add appropriate sales tax.

BM-G

This April, don't miss Harlequin's new Award of
Excellence title from

Award of
Excellence

elusive as the unicorn

*When Eve Eden discovered that Adam
Gardener, successful art entrepreneur, was
searching for the legendary English artist, The
Unicorn, she nervously shied away. The Unicorn's
true identity hit too close to home....*

*Besides, Eve was rattled by Adam's
mesmerizing presence, especially in the light
of the ridiculous coincidence of their names—
and his determination to take advantage of it!
But Eve was already engaged to marry her
longtime friend, Paul.*

*Yet Eve found herself troubled by the different
choices Adam and Paul presented. If only the
answer to her dilemma didn't keep eluding her....*

HP1258-1